Robert Neill Grant

Life of Rev. William Cochrane

Robert Neill Grant

Life of Rev. William Cochrane

ISBN/EAN: 9783337333508

Printed in Europe, USA, Canada, Australia, Japan

Cover: Foto ©Raphael Reischuk / pixelio.de

More available books at **www.hansebooks.com**

LIFE

OF

REV. WILLIAM COCHRANE. D.D.

FOR THIRTY-SIX YEARS PASTOR OF ZION CHURCH, BRANTFORD
AND FOR TWENTY-SIX YEARS CONVENER OF THE HOME
MISSION COMMITTEE OF THE PRESBYTERIAN
CHURCH IN CANADA.

BY

R. N. GRANT.

With Portraits and Illustrations.

TORONTO:

WILLIAM BRIGGS

1899

ILLUSTRATIONS.

		PAGE
WILLIAM COCHRANE	*Frontispiece*	
ZION PRESBYTERIAN CHURCH, BRANTFORD		74
SPECIMEN PAGE FROM MS. OF THE SERMON "IF NEED BE"		90
ADAM SPENCE		162
GEORGE WATT, SEN.		186
WILLIAM WATT, SEN.		210
"VANDUARA" (Dr. Cochrane's Residence in Brantford)		258

CONTENTS.

CHAPTER I.

PAGE

Birth and parentage—School days in Paisley—In business—Enters Glasgow University—Reminiscences by Prof. J. Clark Murray, LL.D., and Rev. Dr. Stewart - - - - - - - - - 9

CHAPTER II.

Voyage to America—New York to Cincinnati—College days in Hanover—College days in Princeton—Licensure by the Presbytery of Madison, Indiana - - 25

CHAPTER III.

Call to the Scotch Church, Jersey City—Ordination and Induction—Successful pastoral work—Marriage—Removal to Brantford - - - - - - 60

CHAPTER IV.

Call to Zion Church, Brantford—Induction—State of the Congregation—Its growth—Labours in other places —Pulpit preparation—Pastoral work—Resolution of Presbytery of Paris - - - - - - - 72

CHAPTER V.

Home Mission work—Appointed Convener of the Home Mission Committee—Work on the three great mission fields : Manitoba—Muskoka—British Columbia —Addresses—Letters—Reports - - - - 104

CONTENTS.

CHAPTER VI.

Various kinds of work—On the press—In the Church Courts—On Commissions—Volumes published—The Pan-Presbyterian Alliance—The Young Ladies' College - - - - - - - - - - - 134

CHAPTER VII.

Dr. Cochrane as a citizen—His first vote in America— Interest in public affairs—His political creed - - 150

CHAPTER VIII.

At his last meeting of the Home Mission Committee— Illness—Sudden death—Funeral services—Addresses by several ministers - - - - - - 156

CHAPTER IX.

In Memoriam—Telegrams, Letters and Resolutions of condolence—Memorial sermon by Dr. McMullen— Reminiscences by Professor Bryce and Dr. McMullen 189

CHAPTER X.

Sermons - - - - - - - - - - 262

LIFE OF WILLIAM COCHRANE.

CHAPTER I.

Birth and parentage—School days in Paisley—In business—
Enters Glasgow University—Reminiscences by Prof. J.
Clark Murray, LL.D., and Rev. Dr. Stewart.

THE Rev. William Cochrane, D.D., was born in
Paisley, Scotland, on the 9th of February, 1831.
His father was from Dalry, Ayrshire, and his mother
from Arran. Her maiden name was McMillan. The
Rev. John McMillan, of Mount Forest, himself an
enthusiastic Arran man, is informed, after making
inquiry, that Dr. Cochrane's mother was a niece of
the late Rev. Angus McMillan, of Arran, a man, Mr.
McMillan says, "of godly fame and character." Of
course, Mr. McMillan thinks that Dr. Cochrane owed
his good qualities mainly to his mother, and that his
mother owed hers to Arran.

William Cochrane went to school when he was four
years of age. Quite likely he was older at four than
most boys are. We have no information in regard to

his school days ; none is needed.   He must have been a bright, breezy, pushing little fellow.   Education has no resources by which a dull, stupid, heavy boy can be developed into a Dr. Cochrane.   The primary schools of Paisley must have given much attention to fundamental work in those days, because at an early age young Cochrane wrote beautifully, handled figures dexterously, and displayed no weakness for originality in spelling.

When twelve years of age he left school and entered the service of Murray & Stewart, booksellers, of Paisley, as message boy.   It is quite safe to say that he could cover more ground in less time than any other message boy in the old town.   Faithful and efficient service brought promotion, and in a few years we find him manager of the business.

In 1853 our young friend came to what he described as the most " agonizing day of his existence."   On the morning of July 11th, of that year, his mother died.   He was well nigh crushed.   His heart cried out, " O God, what shall I answer Thee ?   Teach me, O teach me submission."

Two or three days after the funeral, Mr. Robert Brown, of Cincinnati, an old friend of the family, came to Paisley to visit Mrs. Cochrane.   He was shocked when he heard that she was in her grave. In his own and his brother's name he offered her son ample pecuniary assistance to study for the ministry if he would come to America. Mr. Cochrane hesitated for a considerable time before coming to a conclusion. He wished to become a minister, and he well knew that his mother's prayer had long been that some day her son might occupy the pulpit. But he did not like to leave Paisley, and some of his friends—his minister among the number—were not in favour of his going to America. Perhaps, too, he felt some delicacy in receiving assistance even from so generous and true a friend as Robert Brown. There was no reason why any such feeling should exist, if it did exist. The writer is told, on what he considers excellent authority, that Mr. Robert Brown defrayed the expenses of educating seven Presbyterian ministers. During his student days Mr. Cochrane once discussed the delicate question with Mr. Brown and was assured that the matter was not a personal one. Mr. Brown was working for his Master in this way, and if he did not help William Cochrane at college he would help some other deserving young man. There was nothing more said ; but it ought to be put down here that Robert and Daniel Brown nobly redeemed the promise made that day in Paisley to William Cochrane under the shadow of his sore bereavement.

Prof. J. Clark Murray, LL.D., of McGill University,

a life-long friend of Dr. Cochrane, has kindly contributed the following reminiscences. Interesting
information is also furnished by another friend, Dr.
John Stewart, of Glasgow.

FROM PROF. J. CLARK MURRAY, LL.D.

Of Dr. Cochrane's family I know nothing. I remember, indeed, his mother. Away back in the forties, when
I was a child, I used to see her occasionally. She
was then a widow, living with her son in a house on
Love Street, Paisley, opposite what were then known
as the Hope Temple Gardens, which have since been
presented to the town by the late Mr. Thomas Coats
for a public place of recreation, and are known as the
Fountain Gardens. Dr. Cochrane himself I did not
know till the fifties, when I became a student. He
was then in the bookshop of Mr. Robert Stewart at
the Cross of Paisley, and ultimately became manager
of Mr. Stewart's business. I am not without good
reason in saying that the success of the business at
this time was largely owing to the ability displayed
by young Cochrane in its management.

A bookshop is always an attraction as well as a
necessity to a student, and of the higher class of books
Mr. Stewart usually kept a stock that was indeed
very fair for a provincial town.

It was always easy to spend a pleasant half hour in

looking through the books in his shop, and it was in this occupation that I formed the acquaintance of Dr. Cochrane.

I soon found that he knew books not merely by the outside or by their commercial value.   He spoke of the commodities in which he dealt in the spirit of a student rather than that of a tradesman.   His talk seemed to be attracted to works of a religious or theological nature more than to other departments of literature, though this may have been partly due to his knowledge that I was studying for the ministry. It soon became evident that his heart lay in the work of the Church, and that, if he had seen his way to it, as he did a few years afterwards, he would gladly have devoted himself to that sphere of labour.   This appeared from the active part that he took in the religious life of his native town.

During the controversy which ended in the Disruption of 1843, Dr. Cochrane was, of course, a mere child, and even at the issue he was only twelve years of age.   I take it therefore that, like myself, he found himself in the Free Church, originally at least, not from any independent personal conviction, but from circumstances determined by others.   It is but fair to add that, however sincere his attachment to the Free Church, I cannot recall from the years of our early friendship a single instance of objectionable sectarianism on his part, though it must be remembered that at that time denominational differences were much more pronounced than they are at the present day.

I was not in the least surprised, therefore, when he revisited his native town for the first time (in 1860), to hear him preach in one of the Established Churches, the Abbey Parish church of Paisley. But even in the earlier days his work in connection with the Free Church ran along the lines of a catholic Christianity, not those of denominational controversy. He was connected with the Free Middle Church of Paisley. Its minister, Dr. William Fraser, had indicated that a prominent part of his work would be devoted to the spiritual interests of young men. In this work he was greatly assisted by one of his younger elders, Mr. John Smart, who was then principal of one of the educational institutions in the town, and a man of rare literary and scientific attainments, but whose early death was a severe loss to the cause of education. In this work Dr. Cochrane displayed a keen interest, and took a prominent part in the Young Men's Society, over which Dr. Fraser presided. As the Society was not restricted to adherents of Dr. Fraser's own congregation, I became a member, and in this way found an additional means of enjoying the friendship of Dr. Cochrane.

I owe to the courtesy of Dr. Fraser a copy of his book, "Blending Lights." It is a work of popular apologetics, and enjoyed a good deal of popularity, especially in the United States, about a quarter of a century ago. I fancy it embodies some of the best results of Dr. Fraser's teaching to the young men of Paisley, and conveys a fair idea of the intellectual and spiritual influences by which young Cochrane was trained under the ministry of the author.

Outside of the Free Middle Church, however, Cochrane was also active in religious work. Young Men's Christian Associations were then in their infancy, but about the time of my first acquaintance with Cochrane one was started in Paisley, and he and I became members. I remained in the ranks; he, who was some years my senior, became a prominent office bearer—secretary or president, I forget which. There was another religious society in which I must have met him in those days, though I cannot recall his connection with it so distinctly. It was a Young Men's Sabbath Morning Association. It had several branches throughout the town, which met every Sabbath morning at eight o'clock for a brief devotional exercise and study of the Bible. One member was appointed to read a short essay on the subject of study, and any of the other members, who had given some attention to the subject, were expected to add their reflections. At intervals also—I think once a quarter —a general meeting of all the branches was held at some central place in the town. In all these societies the impression of Dr. Cochrane, which is most prominent in my memory, is connected with the amazing fertility of expression he possessed at a time when most of us are just stammering into the faculty of intelligible public speech. I am sure I have heard, not in a tone of unkindly depreciation, but rather in good-humoured amazement, the remark, " That wee body * Cochrane has a wonnerfu' gift o' the gab."

It is not surprising, with his zeal for religious work, that he should have formed the design of trying to prepare for the ministry in spite of the formidable obstacles by which he was surrounded. Accordingly, two or three years after I had begun my studies, he entered the University of Glasgow. He was able to do this while still attending to his business in Paisley, in consequence of the early hour at which many of the classes in the University met. The Junior Humanity, which he attended, met then, as did several other classes, at half-past seven in the morning. He was thus able to be back at his post in Paisley before the business of the day had fairly begun in the shop. In those days there was only one train in the morning sufficiently early to take us to Glasgow in time

* Everybody is a " body" in Paisley.

to enable us to reach the University by half-past seven; and as it ran in connection with steamers from Belfast and other ports arriving at Greenock, I remember that it was often unreliable in stormy winter weather. This probably explains why young Cochrane sometimes preferred to walk the whole way —fully eight miles from his own home. But to realize his courageous and resolute perseverance it must be borne in mind that, in the northerly and humid climate of Scotland, such a journey has for two or three months to be trudged in complete darkness, and that during the remainder of the winter it is most frequently relieved only by a very grey dawn ushering in a cloudy if not rainy day. As we were not attending the same classes, I rarely met Cochrane at the University, but I have still a very distinct picture of him in my memory as he appeared in those days among the crowds in the quadrangles of the old College building on High Street. As he never remained during the day to join in the rough tussle of the students' out-door life, his toga wore a brand new look and a bright scarlet hue, which contrasted with the dingy red of the tattered garments that fluttered on the backs of most of his fellow students; and while students generally allowed the toga to hang very loosely from the shoulders, as if it were about to slip off behind, I remember seeing him, once or twice at least, with his buttoned close in front as if he had been seeking additional protection against a chilling storm of wind or rain.

Whether Cochrane continued this trying ordeal for more than one session I cannot now remember. In 1854 I went to the University of Edinburgh to continue my philosophical studies under Sir William Hamilton, and I did not see so much of my old friend after that. It must have been about 1853 that a gentleman from the United States—a relative or old friend of the family—came to visit Mrs. Cochrane ; and, on learning of her son's eagerness to enter the ministry, and of the heroic effort he had been making to obtain the necessary education, generously offered to enable him to carry out his wishes, and induced him to migrate with him to his home in the United States. I remember being told at the time all the circumstances connected with this generous act, but I cannot now remember the name of the benefactor. Since that time Dr. Cochrane and I have met often, both in Canada and in Scotland ; but there are others who can tell more of this latter period of his life than I. It will not now, however, be any breach of confidence to mention a proof of the kindly way in which he cherished the associations of his early years.

When the Ladies' College at Brantford was started he wrote to me in very generous terms, urging me to undertake the office of Principal ; and I take it that his action was largely due to the genial memories and sentiments of an old friendship.

FROM DR. JOHN STEWART.

His father died when he was quite young.

HIS MOTHER

was a worthy Christian woman. She was a regular attender at Church, and always took her young boy —an only child—with her. Left with the undivided responsibility of bringing up her son, she nursed him for the Lord, and He gave her her wages. For all her anxieties, prayers, and efforts towards him was she abundantly rewarded. She aimed to stamp on his soft and plastic heart the impress of a godly example. She sheltered his young life under the Mercy-seat. In his infancy she nurtured his soul with the "sincere milk" of love, and in later years with the "strong meat" of knowledge and truth, and God crowned her aims with gladdening success.

HIS CHILDHOOD.

From his earliest years William Cochrane had a liking for the services of the sanctuary. When quite a youth he gave himself with earnestness and ardour to Sabbath School and Church work. By nature he was of a lively temperament and lovable disposition, and as a consequence was greatly beloved by his fellow-workers.

HIS MINISTER.

In the year 1849—when William was eighteen years of age—an event happened which was to powerfully influence all his after life : the Rev. Wm. Fraser (afterwards Dr. Fraser) was ordained minister of the Free Middle Church. The new minister was, after his mother, the most important factor in the formation of Mr. Cochrane's character and career. Indeed, the Rev. Wm. Fraser was one of God's good gifts to Paisley, especially to its young men. Between him and Cochrane there sprang up what can only be called a comradeship—a comradeship which was never broken, however far apart afterwards their spheres of labour lay. As very brothers they laboured at the work of training the youth of Paisley, morally and intellectually.

The wonderful activity and exceptional gifts which Canada was, later on, so largely to profit by, were then displayed in his native town. That readiness in debate, that wonderful gift of oratory, that unfailing courtesy, that indomitable perseverance—afterwards displayed on the wider fields of Presbytery, Synod and Assembly—all shone out at this early stage in connection with his own congregation.   "The child was the father of the man."

IN BUSINESS.

In his boyhood William entered the employment of one of the largest booksellers and printers in Paisley, where, by business capacity, diligence and fidelity, he quite early rose to the onerous and honourable position of manager.   Such was his wide and accurate knowledge of all that concerned the book trade, and his readiness to oblige with information, that the business flourished and the warehouse became a sort of rendezvous for the literary and *elite* of the town.

When his minister, who was a great lover of Natural Science, formed a class to teach "The Relations between Religion and Science," no fewer than three hundred young men joined it, Cochrane amongst them.   Into the work of this class he threw his whole mind, and such was his grasp of the subjects and his readiness of speech, that when Dr. Fraser was necessarily absent—as not unfrequently happened, for he was a popular and much-sought-after man—William was entrusted to conduct the class.   Indeed, his minister treated him as a younger brother, put confidence in him, guided him in his private studies, and confirmed him in his resolution to quit business and become a minister.

HIS EARLY TOILS.

During his student career his was a busy life. It was the wonder of Paisley then, as it was the wonder of Canada in later years, how he overtook all his varied engagements. With a large commercial business to manage ; with various societies, of which he was the mainspring, to prepare for ; with congregational meetings and *soirées* to attend—none of which was supposed to be complete without him— and, in addition, his university work to accomplish, he was doing the work of several men rolled into one; yet you never found him in a hurry, but always with time to spare for any useful work or desired counsel. It was a pleasure to see the neatly attired, scrupulously clean and smiling little man step up to you as brisk as a bee. Such labours would have overtaxed a much more powerful frame than his, had it not been for the lightning speed at which mind and pen moved, and his genuine Paisley pluck. When it is known that in order to reach the Glasgow University he had to travel, sometimes on foot, nearly eight miles and be there at 7.30 a.m., and then return to business—for he still kept his commercial connection— and this for six days in the week, he may well be ranked in the noble band of Scotchmen who, from the humbler ranks and under great difficulties, have fought their way to distinction in various spheres of life and have shed lustre on their native land. Notwithstanding his long sojourn in the United States of America and in Canada ; notwithstanding his new environment and the arduous duties—congregational, denominational and educational duties—which he undertook and faithfully discharged, he never forgot Paisley, but kept up a correspondence with old friends. Not unfrequently he took his summer furlough in his native country—then Paisley was his headquarters. When there he usually preached three times each Sabbath. Indeed, what is said of the tongue, that "its work is its pleasure and its rest is its pain," may be said of him. So often as he preached in Paisley the town was stirred to hear him, so popular was he as a preacher and so beloved as a man. On these visits he was usually the guest of either Provost McGowan or Bailie Dobie. In the evening friends were invited to meet him, and the time was pleasantly spent in rehearsing the sunny memories of fifty years ago.

HIS EARLY PREPARATION FOR HIS FUTURE WORK.

From the preceding epitome of Dr. Cochrane's early years it will be seen how God was, in a way then unknown, preparing him for the great work he was to do. His business training equipped him for the immense amount of business he was called upon to transact as convener of the vast home mission enterprise of Canada. His position as manager of a flourishing warehouse brought him into contact with men in all ranks of society, and so prepared him to be at ease when called to meet and deal with the most exalted in the Dominion. The great diversity of his engagements when young made him the versatile minister he afterwards became.

CHAPTER II.

Voyage to America—New York to Cincinnati—College days in Hanover—College days in Princeton—Licensure by the Presbytery of Madison, Indiana.

ON the 11th day of July, 1854, William Cochrane, then a young man of three-and-twenty, sailed from Glasgow on the steamship *Glasgow* bound for New York. The voyage, which lasted seventeen days, was certainly not without incident. There was a birth and a baptism, two deaths and a burial. There was a fight, and a fire in the steerage, and a narrow escape from collision in a fog on the banks of Newfoundland. The weather was stormy for several days, and young Cochrane seems to have suffered from sea sickness during the greater part of the voyage. On the second day out he writes, " Very sick all day up on deck, but useless;" and on the fourth, "Sick and in bed all day, able to do nothing, say nothing, write nothing, eat nothing, sleep nothing; never got off my pillow." The day following he says, "I lay still, miserable, dull, dejected, downcast, disconsolate. I wish much my friend McKinlay was here to minister to my wants."

Those who knew Mr. William Cochrane in after life will be surprised to read that he "lay still." Keeping still never was his strong point, and as a matter of fact he did not keep still very long on this voyage, though he was more or less sea-sick nearly all the time. The very day on which he "lay still" he managed in some way to find out that at twelve o'clock the vessel had sailed 163 miles in twenty-four hours. Sailing at the same rate he estimated that it would take sixteen days to reach New York. This prospect he described by one word and two exclamation points, "Horrible!!" Matters were not mended the next day when it was ascertained that the vessel had sailed only eighty-five miles. This rate of speed he characterized as "Miserable!"

Like almost every other intelligent man that ever crossed the Atlantic, young Cochrane expected to do a good deal of reading on board ship. His expectations were not realized. Nearing Newfoundland he says, "With sickness and one thing and another I get no reading at all. Attempted 'Plurality of Worlds,' but failed; attempted the 'Poets of America and England,' but failed; am now at 'Sketches by Boz,' but am tired of them. I should like to have Scott's 'Old Mortality,' which I have not got all through yet."

Though not able to read much on board ship, William Cochrane was not the young man to allow seventeen days to pass without doing work of some kind. He kept an accurate account of each day's sailing, and satisfied himself each day as to the "whereabouts" of the ship. Only one day was he too sick to get the latitude and longitude, and he worried over the unknown "whereabouts" in much the same way as long years afterwards he used to worry over a deficit in the funds of the Home Mission Committee.

The first evening on board ship passengers usually try to solve the question "Who is who?" which, being interpreted, means "Who are your berthmates?" William Cochrane was much pleased to find that one of his berthmates was a "U. P. preacher named Glassford." The Mr. Glassford here referred to was the Rev. P. Glassford, who afterwards became pastor of the Presbyterian church in Vaughan, Ont. On the removal of Mr. Cochrane to Brantford, in 1862, the acquaintanceship formed on board the steamer *Glasgow* ripened into friendship that continued until Mr. Glassford's death.

On the fifth day at sea an incident occurred which shows the invincible love of Scotchmen for ecclesiastical discussion. Mr. Cochrane himself must tell the story: "Wind still prevailing. The sea running mountains high. Never saw anything like it. Fearful to look out, contemplating the consequences. Glassford and I kept beds all day. A little dry toast for breakfast, sago and raisins for dinner, and a little dry toast for tea. Glassford and I, poor mortals, lay and chatted about Church and State. We discussed all the notables of the past and present centuries—Dr. Chalmers, Dr. McGill, Dickson, Cairns, McDougall, Brewster, etc. Got some good hints as to study." Small wonder that William Cochrane became Moderator of the Canadian General Assembly. A talented, industrious, ambitious young man of twenty-three, who can, while suffering from sea-sickness, and living on dry toast, discuss problems of Church and State while the ship rolls and the waves run " mountains high," is very likely to rise to any position in the gift of a self-governed Church.

Toward the end of the voyage he became acquainted with two gentlemen who were going to Madison, near Cincinnati, and who were well acquainted with the friends in Cincinnati who had agreed to help him in his efforts to secure an education for the ministry. No one who knew Dr. Cochrane need be told that these gentlemen were asked leading questions about Cincinnati and its surroundings. He also met a young lady from the same part of the country. From these three, he says, he got " some useful information about Hanover and Oxford Colleges." Nearer the end of the voyage he had a " long chat " with the young lady, in which she gave

him " full particulars of Cincinnati," and also informed
him that he would " never see a Scottish Sabbath in
America," a prediction which he afterwards found
fulfilled to the letter.

If the discussion with Mr. Glassford, while both lay
in their berths suffering from sea-sickness, showed
young Cochrane's inborn love for ecclesiastical affairs,
another incident brought out in bold relief one of the
strongest traits of his character.   One of his fellow-
passengers was a young companion named Kerr.
Kerr stood the siege bravely at first, and was able to
read the " Plurality of Worlds," and enjoy himself
generally, while Cochrane was confined to his berth
unable to hold his own in more senses than one.
After a time Kerr succumbed and Cochrane had to
take care of him.   " Poor Kerr," he says, " is suffering
more than I am from sickness and exhaustion.   He
has acted very foolishly in taking one dose after
another until his system is quite reduced.   I am
doing all I can to encourage him to eat and to quit
taking medicine.   He has lost heart entirely and is
quite depressed in spirits.   I strive always to keep up
my spirits, though my prospects are in the main, I
think, worse than his.   It is good to rely on providence."   Here we have an explanation of the question so often asked, " How did Dr. Cochrane keep his
hold on Zion Church, Brantford, for thirty-six years,

though he did so much outside work, and was so much from home?" He kept his hold mainly by his self-denying efforts to help the poor, the sick and the dying. There were few years, in that long and successful pastorate, when he did not help parishioners who needed help less than he needed it himself.

On the 26th of the month the pilot came on board and got a hearty welcome. Mr. Cochrane, with his usual plainness of speech, describes him as "an out-and-out Yankee, both in person and dress." Next day land was seen, and about nine o'clock in the evening the *Glasgow* landed at her dock. There were many happy meetings, and at least one friend came down to meet the young man from Paisley. "Shaw"—perhaps some old Paisley boy—"came on board and fairly astounded us by his Yankee dress and moustache." Those who had homes went to them, but the future pastor of Zion Church, Brantford, "at eleven, turned into bed," but, as we can easily understand, "not to sleep."

Next morning he was up at four o'clock and on deck, perhaps on the assumption that a man who succeeds in the United States must rise early; but more likely because he could not sleep. During the day he had his first experiences of business in the new world, and they were such as to convince him that the "Yankees are a knowing set." "Duncan and I paid 6/6 for our breakfast—a regular take in; and then the taking of my baggage cost me I don't know how many dollars." In the afternoon he had his watch repaired, and the bill amounted to 14/. Not being accustomed to count in American currency or to pay American prices, he considered their business operations "horribly vexatious!" No doubt they were, though he was only one of many thousand emigrants who had similar experiences on their arrival in the new world. All the others, however, could not express their feelings under the fleecing operation as vigorously as this young man from Paisley did when he wrote "horribly vexatious!"

The next five or six days were spent in attending to some matters of business, sight-seeing, and calling upon former friends and acquaintances. There were many young people from Paisley and Glasgow in New York, and Mr. Cochrane seemed to think that he should call upon those of them that he knew and see how they were getting on in the new world. Sight-seeing in New York in July weather is no easy matter, especially for one who has been accustomed to a cool climate, and whose wardrobe consists of heavy Old Country clothes. Young Cochrane, however, was equal to the emergency. He had learned that "the New Yorkers are all early astir," and he rose at six o'clock each day and got ready for business. He tramped the city until his feet swelled so that he could scarcely walk, but with that invincible energy which characterized his whole life he stuck to the sight-seeing until he got a fair idea of New York. The size of the place and the rush and roar of business greatly impressed him. The day after he landed he writes : " This is an awful city, without doubt. I never saw such stir and variety all my life. It seems endless in extent. Unless guarded, one in a few minutes would be perfectly lost."

The young man, however, did not get lost. During the next few days he visited many places of interest, and no doubt learned much about the great city in which he was many years afterwards well known and had many friends. His dislike for New York business, however, was not lessened by the fact that the custom house people made him pay eighteen dollars of duty on some silks that he was taking to friends in Cincinnati. To a Paisley free trader the custom house was repulsive. As he saw the eighteen dollars vanish he gave vent to his feelings by describing the transaction as "most ridiculous." In similar circumstances even fairly good men sometimes use harsher terms.

Our young friend spent only one Sabbath in New York at this time, but one was quite enough to show the influence of environment even upon young men of strong convictions and high principle. In Paisley

the Sabbath was William Cochrane's busiest day.
Besides the regular Sabbath services, which he never
missed, he taught in the Sabbath School, attended
prayer-meeting, and was engaged the whole day in
worship or in some kind of Christian work. His in-
tentions were good in New York. His programme
was to hear Dr. Cheever and Gardiner Spring, but he
did not know where to find their churches. Friends
asked him to go out into the country and see a friend
of theirs, and he went. The day was spent pleasantly, but he says it was "not quite like a Sabbath. I
think there was a letting down of Christian principle ;
but oh, the flesh and blood are weak!" In the evening of this first Sabbath in America his feelings were
not pleasant. "I should have been much better had
I attended church. I never knew any good to follow
a carelessly observed Sabbath."

Early on the following Thursday morning Mr.
Cochrane left for Cincinnati, the city that was to be
his home for the next five years. Robert and Daniel
Brown, the friends who had interested themselves in
aiding him to study for the ministry, were prosperous
merchants of Cincinnati, and belonged to a group of
prosperous Scotch people who took a warm interest
in the young man from Paisley who had come to
America to prepare himself for the pulpit. One good
lady had a habit of slipping gold pieces into his hand

when he said good-bye at the close of each vacation, and others helped and encouraged him in many ways. How much the Presbyterian Church in Canada owes to these friends in Cincinnati who helped William Cochrane to become a minister of the Gospel, and more particularly to Robert and Daniel Brown, will never be known until the great final reckoning takes place.

The journey from New York to Cincinnati was a much more serious matter in those days than it has since become. Mr. Cochrane thus describes it:

"Started at seven Thursday morning in the cars and travelled to Dunkirk, which we reached at eleven at night; changed cars and took the Buffalo train to Erie; changed again and took the Erie cars to Cleveland, which we reached at five Friday morning; breakfasted in Cleveland and started for Columbus, which we reached at one and started for Cincinnati. When we arrived Robert Brown was at the station to receive us."

Needless to say there was a warm welcome, not only from the Browns but from many of their Scotch friends. The first evening was spent in "talking over old stories and joking." The following day he hunted up some old friends, by whom he says he was "entertained most sumptuously."

Of course William Cochrane could not be long in

any place without showing his interest in church matters, and his second evening was spent at choir practice in the church to which the Browns belonged. And thus did the future Moderator of the General Assembly of the Presbyterian Church in Canada begin his ecclesiastical career in America.

The first Sabbath in Cincinnati was a busy one and impressed our young friend with the fact that even good people in Cincinnati did not keep the Sabbath in the way he had seen it kept in Paisley. In the morning he went to Sabbath School and taught a class, the lesson being Paul's shipwreck. At eleven he heard Dr. Biggs, pastor of the church that Daniel and Robert Brown attended, who preached on the words, "I am the way, the truth and the life." The services were enjoyed, but the Cincinnati Sabbath was a revelation. "On my way to and from church witnessed a great many shops open—tobacconists, confectioners, grocers and drapers. Others had only the half door opened as if half conscience smitten; others, again, were sitting here and there, reading, lounging and turning over the papers; others whistling, and playing the organ, the violin, and the piano. In fact one of the teachers in the school, at its dismissal, whistled a smart air as if it had been a Psalm tune. Such is a Cincinnati Sabbath!"

In the afternoon he attended Dr. Biggs' Bible class,

3

which he thought very interesting, and in the evening went with Daniel Brown to a Methodist Camp Meeting, four miles out of the city, which was interesting and something more. " The roads were very dusty, and I am sure we met in with nearly a hundred vehicles. It reminded me of the way to the Paisley race course." Though the Sabbath driving and the living in tents did not come up to the Paisley standard, still young Cochrane was compelled to admit that there was something good in that camp meeting. " Here and there, on a sort of election hustings, preachers *ad infinitum* held forth to their respective audiences. We heard one for half an hour and a very good preacher he certainly was. They appear most earnest men, thoroughly alive to the momentous interests of eternity and deeply desirous for the conversion of souls."

Mr. Cochrane's Cincinnati friends had not yet decided what college he should attend, but as Hanover was the nearest his attention was directed to that institution. He got a copy of the curriculum, and, in his own terse words, " conned " it over. The conclusion he came to was that " it will be just as hard as Glasgow." To make things sure, he and Robert Brown started to Hanover to see the authorities of the college personally. A night's sail on the Ohio, which Mr. Cochrane enjoyed immensely, brought them to Madison, and an hour's drive to the college. Here he was mortified to learn that his course would not be much shorter than it would have been in the Old Country. " I now find that so far from shortening my studies by coming to America, I have made a woeful mistake. After four or five years in Hanover—four at least—I must go for three to a theological seminary. I feel quite down-cast, but I must now do my best. I say 'must,' for I cannot brook the idea of turning back to Scotland so soon." As events turned out, the course was a little shortened, though near its close the young man himself often thought it was not long enough. The length of the course, however, was not the only trouble now. The entrance examination required Algebra, and though William Cochrane knew a thousand things that average matriculants do not know, he knew little or nothing about Algebra. He had thirteen books " to profess " and five or six weeks to prepare for examination. He thought he could manage with all the other subjects, but he was very skeptical about the Algebra. Back he came to Cincinnati and plunged into study with all the energy that characterized his efforts in after life. He rose at six in the morning, revised his Latin and Greek, which he certainly did not need to do, and paid little or no attention to Algebra, which he needed very much. During these weeks he had repeated and severe attacks of depression, which he thought arose from want of confidence in God. He could not understand why a man who had confidence in his Heavenly Father should feel so weary and lonely as he did at times. A sudden change of climate, too many hours of study, a lack of regular and sufficient exercise, added to occasional fits of home-sickness, no doubt caused the depression in so far as it was produced by any external cause. To the end of his days, however, he was subject to severe attacks of depression, and it may be that a natural tendency first manifested itself during these weeks in Cincinnati. He was constantly haunted with the fear that he would not be able to enter the Freshman's class at Hanover. "I must confess beginning to feel very lonely; but what can be done? Were I sure of getting into the Freshman's class I would get up in the spirits, but I fear it much." To counteract the weariness and despondency and "to relieve the tedium and dryness of classical studies," he read the life of McCheyne and the Epistle to the Romans. The remedy was admirable in itself, but whether it could meet all the troubles of the patient was another question. The difference between the heat of August in Cincinnati and the cool air of Paisley could not be lessened by reading McCheyne's Memoirs, nor could even the Epistle to the Romans strengthen a bodily frame that was weak and abnormally sensitive.

During these weeks in Cincinnati young Cochrane finely illustrated the truth that an earnest man can always find his work. He taught in the Sabbath School, took part in the prayer meeting, and made himself generally useful in the Church with which his friends were connected. The Sabbath School he did not altogether like, and his comments may be of use to some engaged in Sabbath School work. On the second Sabbath he writes : " To Sabbath School at 9 —am not at all satisfied with their mode of conducting. There is a formality about it that deprives the exercises of all serious impression on the children's minds. So I judge, at least."

A few days before leaving Cincinnati for Hanover the Sacrament of the Lord's Supper was dispensed in the Church his friends attended. The occasion was a solemn one for William Cochrane and his mind would wander back to Paisley. At the table he fixed his thoughts on the promise, " I will never leave thee ; I will never forsake thee." During the whole of his college life he blamed himself because he had not a Christian experience like that of Robert Murray McCheyne. The young man—fatherless, motherless, homeless, a stranger in a strange land and dependent mainly on his friends—who fixes his mind on the promise, " I will never leave thee," may not be a Mc-Cheyne, but he certainly is on the right path. That promise on which he rested his soul at his first communion in America was well kept through all his journeyings until that Monday evening, fourty-four years afterwards, when William Cochrane breathed his last in his own home in Brantford.

COLLEGE DAYS IN HANOVER.

Monday, the eighteenth day of September, found William Cochrane on board the steamer on his way to Hanover, all his worldly goods in his trunk. The boat arrived in Madison too late for him to drive out to Hanover, and he stayed over night in a Madison hotel. The drive of a few miles from the river port, Madison, to Hanover is usually described as picturesque, but there was nothing of that kind about it the day our young friend arrived at the institution in which he was to be a prominent figure in less than three years. He entered Hanover amidst a storm of rain, and three years afterwards left in a storm of applause. But he must be allowed to describe his entrance himself. " Found no conveyance to Hanover till the afternoon, and engaged a buggy at a dollar and a half to go down. It came on a perfect torrent on the way down, and what with wetness and a miserable slow horse and having to take a longer road than intended, our condition was truly miserable. Reached Hanover about 11, drenched into the skin. I was almost again at the point of despair and almost wished to be back again in Paisley. Put up at a sort of hotel called the —— House, a miserable hovel indeed, and dressed afresh, after which I set off for college."

The visit to the college did not last long, for in the afternoon we find Mr. Cochrane in search of board and lodging. The boarding houses of Hanover were not by any means to his taste. In fact they appeared "most miserable to one who, though not accustomed to grandeur, had for years been accustomed to ordinary gentility." After a long and tedious search he found one "which though by no means nice, must do for a little."

Next day the entrance examination took place. Mr. Cochrane was well prepared in Latin, and specially well in Greek, but he knew almost nothing about Algebra. After some hesitation the Faculty allowed him to matriculate on condition that he should omit Greek in part for the first session and give special attention to mathematics. The unwisdom of cast-iron regulations in educational matters is shown by this examination. Had the letter of the law been strictly enforced, Dr. Cochrane's invaluable labours in the Church of Christ would undoubtedly have been lost. He was in no mood to stand a disappointment. His health was poor, his spirits low, and even after the fear of rejection was past, the most he hoped for was "to make out a quarter at least."

For the first few weeks he found the work hard enough. Mathematics, he thought, would "tax the patience of an angel." His dislike for that subject was not lessened by his feelings towards the professor in the Mathematical Department. "Thomson, the Mathematical Professor, is the most austere man of the lot. I tremble and hesitate and stumble in his presence more than all the others." A few days after matriculation he writes: "These three days have been days of such unceasing toil that I have not had a moment's time to write or do anything but study. The day may be divided something in this fashion: studying and reciting, 16½ hours; sleeping, 6; eating, 1½. This is a shocking arrangement."

The work was very hard because it was not the kind of work that William Cochrane had been trained for doing. His had been mainly a business training. He had learned more about the book trade in Murray & Stewart's than the Faculty of Hanover ever knew; but a knowledge of the book trade was of no use when he was asked to demonstrate a proposition in Euclid. He had read Hugh Miller and Macaulay— had revelled in their works many a morning and evening in Paisley—but these literary giants did not help him to solve an equation. Like many another good student, William Cochrane suffered at the beginning of his college course, not because he had no knowledge, but because his knowledge was not of the kind needed.

On the second Sabbath of the session he had a severe attack of home-sickness and a bright vision of Paisley. "Sitting alone, my thoughts again reverted homeward. I thought of the glorious Sabbaths they enjoy—the peace and happiness and tranquillity of all around. I could picture out the congregation sitting under Mr. Fraser, each family in their particular seat. I could, in memory, place myself in the Morning Association Sabbath School and class and remember the joyous hours I experienced among them. But these days are gone, alas, it may be never to return. But why should I repine or murmur? My God has been gracious to me in the midst of all my vicissitudes. He has guided me hitherto, will He not do so still? I still anticipate seeing Scotland and the Middle Church and there proclaiming, as an ambassador for Christ, the words of eternal life. If such should ever come to pass it will more than repay all present and subsequent fatigue."

This very thing did come to pass six years afterwards. On the afternoon of July 8th, 1860, the Rev. Wm. Cochrane, B.A., pastor of the Scotch Presbyterian Church, Jersey City, preached in the Free Middle

Church, Paisley. His text was Luke xvi. 31. The preacher had hard work to conceal his emotions, and when his mother's old friends gathered round him at the close of the service some of them did not succeed in concealing theirs.

Midway between the opening of the session and the Christmas holidays our young friend's affairs began to brighten. He rose at six—sometimes at five—worked hard, and in Hanover, as in every other place, hard work soon began to tell. There was something about him that attracted attention, and Faculty and students alike began to think that the young bookseller from Paisley was a student that had to be considered. There were two or three societies in the college, and it need hardly be said that William Cochrane soon took an active part in their work and management. In Paisley he had been a prominent figure in various associations, and his experience and business habits soon brought him to the front in the students' societies in Hanover. About six weeks after matriculation his friends ran him against a senior for the office of critic in one of the societies, and the candidates got equal votes. The junior very properly then retired, no doubt quite satisfied with his display of popularity and strength. This was his first contest, but by no means his last. For the next three years he was a leading spirit in these societies, and though not always successful in his elections and other undertakings, everybody recognized him as a potent factor in college life.

The experience he had gained in speaking and writing in the Church societies in Paisley now became useful. He often acted as critic and took part in many debates. There were some good debates in Hanover in those days, but the young man from Paisley was always to the front, win or lose. He carefully noted the effect of his own speeches, and tried hard to avoid errors in delivery which he thought he detected. Quite frequently his criticism of his efforts was that he had spoken "too vehemently," and he tried hard to keep his vehemence in check, a task in which, even to the end of life, he was not always quite successful. He had some good pieces which he recited in vigorous style, and when the programme at a society meeting proved too short, or the meeting became dull, there was sometimes a call for Cochrane, and he never failed to give a recitation that "brought down the house." One of his favourite pieces was the "Spanish Champion." At an evening party, or a meeting of students—in Hanover, or Madison, or Cincinnati—the "Spanish Champion" was always in order and always sure of hearty applause. Spanish champions are not as popular on the banks of the Ohio now as they were when William Cochrane used to "declaim"—as he called it—in Hanover.

Society work, however, was not allowed to interfere with Mr. Cochrane's studies. At the examination held immediately before Christmas in his first session he made a hundred in each of four leading subjects ; ninety-eight was his lowest, and his average ninety-nine and three-fifths. This splendid record was made in spite of frequent attacks of illness. He suffered at times from severe pain in the chest, which made him fear that he was on "the straight road to consumption." This pain in the chest followed him to the very end of his life.

Perhaps the most important feature of this term was his increased hopefulness. One day, about a month before Christmas, he "got confused" in the class room and "failed utterly," as he thought, in mathematics. Instead of allowing the failure to depress him, as he certainly would have done earlier in the session, he wrote : "I must redeem myself next week—am determined not to let failure dishearten me." Failure that makes a student, or any other kind of a man, resolve to redeem himself is not an unmixed evil.

The long looked for graduation day came in August, 1857. Hanover had a summer session, and he had studied three years continuously with the exception of a short vacation in spring and in autumn and a few days at Christmas. During these vacations, which were spent with his friends in Cincinnati, he studied part of almost every day, and at this time, as well as throughout the whole of his life, he always kept some books about him for general reading. During the latter part of his course he taught a class in New Testament Greek with marked success. His final examinations were very good, and his appearances in the commencement exercises were such as to attract general attention. All is well that ends well, and though our friend thought at the beginning of his course that his prospects were dark enough, he made his mark in Hanover, and when he left, many friends, his professors included, predicted a bright future for the young man from Paisley.

The years during which Mr. Cochrane attended Hanover College were eventful, and some of the events raised more than a ripple in college life. The Crimean War was then at its height and public opinion in the United States was largely in favour of Russia. Anti-British feeling occasionally manifested itself in Hanover College, and the representative from Paisley had hard work to control himself. A clergyman of considerable local standing delivered a lecture in the college in which he eulogized Russia, and, by implications at least, denounced the Allies. A student, of course, was not allowed to reply, but Mr. Cochrane vowed that if he could meet the lecturer outside he would give him something to think about.

The Crimean War, however, was not the only event that was then agitating the public mind. The storm that burst upon the country in the Civil War was rapidly gathering. The fight for and against slavery was becoming fierce, and it was as fierce in Hanover College as elsewhere. It goes unsaid that the Paisley student was a pronounced anti-slavery man. In his opinion there was no question to be discussed. Slavery was a "curse," an unmitigated, unrelieved curse, and he could not understand how anybody could take any other view of the question. It was a "hellish invention," and there was nothing more to be said. To the Southern student who offered to prove by Scripture quotation that slavery was right, his only answer was "If you can, I'll turn infidel in a week."

An incident occurred during one of his visits home which greatly intensified his hatred against the "peculiar institution," as slavery was at that time frequently called. At one of the ports on the Ohio a slave girl, recently purchased, was dragged, shrieking, on board the steamer by her owner, and William Cochrane saw the sickening sight and heard her frantic cries. To a young Scotchman accustomed to breathe the free air of Paisley and Glasgow, such an exhibition was simply hellish. His British blood was fired, and he denounced slavery in season and out of season. One of his favourite pieces for declamation was the "Sumner Outrage," and he allowed no opportunity to pass without giving the college societies the benefit of that recitation. At an evening party in Covington he was asked for a recitation, and though the gentlemen present were nearly all Kentucky men, he favored them with the " Sumner Outrage," delivered in his best style. Some of the "bloods" were furious, but the Paisley man showed no white feather. His own opinion was, that if he had been a little farther south he would have gone home wearing a coat of tar and feathers—if he got home at all.

After graduation two weeks were spent in Cincinnati making farewell visits to his friends and preparing for Princeton. It was at this time that Dr. Cochrane preached his first sermon. Dr. T. G. Smith —now of Kingston, Ont.—was then pastor of the Fourth Presbyterian Church of Cincinnati. He had frequently met Mr. Cochrane when the latter was spending his vacations in the city, and had taken quite a friendly interest in him. Naturally enough, the pastor of the Fourth Church asked his young friend to preach for him, which Mr. Cochrane did. The text was I Corinthians i. 22, and the sermon fifty minutes long—quite long enough for a first sermon, delivered on an August evening. Though a young preacher at this time, Mr. Cochrane was a shrewd observer of things ecclesiastic. Writing of a church in Cincinnati—not Dr. Smith's—in which there was trouble on the "choir question," he says : " I never saw such a church for continual strifes. If the minister pleases, the singer don't; if the singer does, the minister don't ; if both these suit, the session is wrong. I pray heaven to watch over them and keep them united." Unfortunately, congregations of that kind are not confined to Cincinnati.

COLLEGE DAYS IN PRINCETON.

Having spent a pleasant fortnight with his friends in Cincinnati, Mr. Cochrane started for Princeton, and got his first view of the great institution on the evening of the first day of September. On this evening he seems to have had one of his old attacks of depression, though in a much milder form than in former years. He says : " My landing to-night all alone and all unknown at Princeton reminds me of this time three years ago at Hanover. But why give way to childish melancholy. The same God that prospered me there can continue His kindness here. What shall I render unto Him for all His past goodness ? "

William Cochrane was a man of faith, but he was also a strong believer in the use of means. " In the absence of all other friends," he tells us, " he struck up a conversation with the coloured waiter and the coloured barber of the hotel in which he stayed over night ; gave each a little additional perquisite, and then proceeded to get from them some little items about the seminary and college." No doubt he found the items useful.

The next day our friend moved into the seminary and called on Drs. Hodge, Green and McGill. Dr. McGill he thought "a very gentlemanly man, of a most lovable disposition and very obliging to students." Drs. Hodge and Green he found " friendly enough, but very reserved." The students he met gave him " the idea of being very aristocratic and unsociable," a very natural idea, perhaps, for a young man who had for three years been accustomed to the free and easy ways of the West.

On the following day the matriculation exercises took place. Dr. Hodge presided, Dr. McGill engaged in prayer, and Dr. Green read the constitution and regulations of the seminary. After pledging themselves to obey the rules, to behave properly and to study faithfully, the students signed the register. The second name to go down was the one that stood for thirty-six years at the head of the list of members of the Home Mission Committee of the Presbyterian Church in Canada.

The opening lecture of the session was by Dr. Green, and the account given of it shows the ability

4

of the professor and the aptitude of the student in taking notes. The subject was, "The Superiority of Theological over all other Science." According to Mr. Cochrane's report the Doctor handled his subject in this masterly way: Theology superior as regards—

I. Its theme.

II. Its profitable character.

III. Its relationship to other branches of knowledge.

IV. Its evidence.

Manifestly, the idea that theology is not a science at all had not reached Princeton at that time.

On the first Sabbath forenoon he heard Dr. Hodge preach on Eph. i. 19. The sermon he describes as "strongly Calvinistic, read for the most part, but delivered in a manner that by its affectionate and winning way enchained all the hearers."

That afternoon our friend seems to have been in an unusually good frame of mind. As he sat in his room he gave way to these reflections: "I think that if anywhere human agency can accomplish anything, it is at Princeton. Every means seems to be used for bringing us to a sense of our position. A holy atmosphere seems to encircle the grounds to-day, and by the hymns and prayers that are heard in almost every student's room, one would almost imagine that we are as near heaven and a heavenly frame as one can expect on this side of the grave. Oh, God, send down the Spirit into my own soul to quicken me in divine things and deaden me to the things of time. In the afternoon read my Bible and devoted some time to reflections and self-examination—a fearfully humiliating, but at the same time profitable, work."

The course of study in Princeton he did not find particularly difficult. There was much to be done, but he worked hard. His studies in Hanover had been arranged mainly with a view to a theological course, and some of the ground had already been gone over. He was now fairly on the way to the pulpit; the dream of his boyhood was soon to become a fact, and William Cochrane was perhaps happier than he ever had been at any past period of his life.

The classes he attended were taught by Drs. Hodge, Green, Alexander and McGill. Personal contact with such men was one of the formative influences that Mr. Cochrane needed and needed much at this particular time. His temperament was naturally aggressive; he was flushed with his success at Hanover; he had been accustomed for three years to the free methods of Western life, and the dignified reserve of such men as Hodge and Green had a most salutary influence upon his character.

The preaching, too, was of the highest order. Besides the professors, representative ministers from all parts of the country preached in the seminary, and Mr. Cochrane was often powerfully impressed by their pulpit efforts. The Sabbath afternoon conference, conducted usually by Drs. Hodge, Alexander, Green, and McGill, was also a powerful agency in moulding his character and firing him with zeal for his future work. Good sermons in Cincinnati and Hanover often led him to compare the preacher to Macnaughton of Paisley. The services in the seminary usually led him to think about himself and his relation to his Saviour.

In December of his first session, Mr. Cochrane delivered his first sermon in the seminary. Dr. McGill characterized it as "very animated, and a style of oratory that might be expected from one born in Ireland, with a Western education." The preacher had two theories with regard to this criticism of his first seminary effort. One was that Dr. McGill was a poor judge of dialect and unable to distinguish between an Irishman and a man born in Paisley. The other was that the good doctor intended it all for a joke. Old Princetonians who read these pages must decide for themselves which theory was correct.

The summer of 1858 was spent in Cincinnati. On his way west he visited the Falls of Niagara, and was greatly pleased to set his foot once more on British soil. During this vacation he preached every Sabbath, supplying for a considerable time the congregation, of Montgomery, in the vicinity of Cincinnati. This was his first continuous work in any congregation, and he did it with an amount of enthusiasm that soon put life into the congregation.

In May of this summer he visited Hanover, passed an examination before the Presbytery of Madison, and had subjects prescribed for examination for license next year. In August he again visited his old friends in Hanover and Madison, and preached several times in Madison. This was his last summer in the West, and he keenly felt parting from his many friends. Nineteen years afterwards he and Mrs. Cochrane and their daughter Mary spent their vacation in the places on the Ohio River that had become much endeared to the Doctor in the early days of his life in America. They visited friends in Cincinnati, Madison, Hanover, Louisville, Covington, and everywhere got a hearty welcome. The Doctor preached, of course, every Sabbath, and the old friends of his student days were delighted to hear him. One sermon was delivered to the students and faculty of Hanover, and we can easily imagine that the preacher had some peculiar sensations during that service. Among the old friends that he visited he did not forget to call on the good woman he had boarded with during his college days. She had become quite blind, but her heart was still warm, and she welcomed her old boarder by giving a motherly kiss to him and his good lady. The strongest feature of Dr. Cochrane's character was his kindness to the aged, the poor, and the helpless, and it is not a matter of wonder that he valued as highly the welcome of this good old friend as he did the welcome of any other friend on the Ohio.

The second day of September found him in his room in Princeton arranging his books and getting ready for seminary work. His room-mates, he considered, had "not much taste in these things," and the duty of keeping the room in order always devolved upon himself. Anybody who ever saw the inside of Dr. Cochrane's study will have no difficulty in coming to the conclusion that the standard set up for the room-mates was much too high for average mortals.

The session upon which he was now entering proved to be one of unusual profit and enjoyment. He kept well abreast of his work, and thoroughly enjoyed all his classes except Church History. He had not, or imagined he had not, any capacity for remembering "dates and events," but his examination at the close of the session showed that he had greatly exaggerated his incapacity for studying Church History, if any such incapacity existed. He was an active member of the Chalmers Club and of the Society of Enquiry. The services conducted by the professors and visiting ministers, the Sabbath afternoon conferences, as well as the prayer-meetings in the seminary, were to him sources of great spiritual profit. At the close of a missionary prayer-meeting, held one Sabbath evening in his own room, he writes : " It was a delightful meeting—altogether this has been a precious Sabbath. I feel that I have been more in the Spirit to-day than usual ; and oh, if I could but continue! How precious to be near heaven in mind, if not in actual presence. Lord, purify me more and more, and make me feel my inability to do anything aright of myself !"

During this session he preached quite frequently, but it is impossible at this distance in time and space to ascertain anything accurate about his early pulpit efforts around Princeton. In Montgomery, where he preached during the previous summer, he certainly had been successful in stirring up the people. All we know about his ability to please the more fastidious taste of the East—and at that time it certainly was more fastidious—is that during his last session a congregation in Jersey City frequently heard him, and a few weeks after the session closed asked him to be their pastor.

During his course in Princeton, Mr. Cochrane was

under the care of the Presbytery of Madison, Indiana. In February he made a flying visit to his old home, and after examination by the Presbytery, was, on the sixteenth day of February, in the year eighteen hundred and fifty-nine, duly licensed to preach the glorious Gospel of the blessed God. His feelings on that eventful day are best described by himself: "And thus did I at last attain what I had desired from my infancy, to preach the glorious Gospel of the Cross. Oh, my God, now that thy vows are upon me, may I be enabled to act differently than in the past: more diligent to win souls; more earnest in the cause of Christ; inflamed with greater zeal for the kingdom of the Redeemer. Oh, direct my every step, sustain me in every duty, comfort me in times of despondency, and help me in all my conduct to adorn the doctrines of my Saviour by a walk and conversation becoming the Gospel. If I fall soon in the fight, may a better soldier be raised up to carry on the work."

Returning to Princeton, he studied faithfully to the end of the session, passed his examinations successfully in every department, and on the twenty-sixth day of April left the institution he so much loved to begin the career of influence and usefulness that closed so suddenly nearly forty years afterwards in Brantford, Ontario.

The energetic youth whose footsteps we have followed since he left Paisley is now the Rev. William Cochrane, B.A. During his collegiate course he was a good student, but he was much more than a student. Rarely, if ever, did he fail to attend the prayer-meeting wherein he might be, and he usually took part in the service. He was a most successful Sabbath School teacher, and perhaps the most joyful hour of his college days was the one in which several members of the Sabbath School class he taught in Princeton professed their faith in Christ.

Dr. Cochrane had little patience with idleness or slipshod work in the church. It ought to be remembered that when he was a mere lad in Paisley and an over-worked student in Hanover, he did what he could to advance Christ's cause. His early life was a fine illustration of the fact that an earnest man will work where he is and as he is.

CHAPTER III.

Call to the Scotch church, Jersey City—Ordination and induction—Successful pastoral work—Marriage—Removal to Brantford.

DURING his last session at Princeton, Mr. Cochrane preached quite frequently. One Sabbath, in November, he supplied the pulpit of a friend in New York City. A number of men from the Scotch church of Jersey City were present, and at the close of the service asked him to preach in their church, which was then vacant, and on the look-out for a pastor. He agreed to do so, but not as a candidate. On the second day of January he made his first appearance in the pulpit which was soon to become his own. His texts were 2 Corinthians v. 20, and Psalms xlvi. 1. The impression made must have been good, for negotiations soon afterwards began which ended in his settlement. At first his desire was merely to supply the pulpit for the summer months. About this time he had a visit from his good friend, Mr. Robert Brown, of Cincinnati. Mr. Brown was opposed to anything that might lead to a permanent settlement in Jersey City.   The principal grounds of opposition were that Mr. Cochrane was not strong enough to undertake the work of a city congregation, and that his lungs were too weak for the air of the sea coast.   He had made arrangements for having his young friend spend another vacation with him in Cincinnati, and he could find work for him in Montgomery and in a vacancy in Cincinnati.   Mr. Brown was perhaps right, but having stated his views he generously told his friend to exercise his own judgment in the matter.   Mr. Cochrane went on supplying the congregation, and they called him.   He was sorely puzzled as to the course which he should pursue, and earnestly prayed for divine guidance.   There were some reasons why he would have liked to study for another session, and one or two strong reasons why he should accept the call.   In some way or other he had come to the conclusion that " Scotch congregations in America are ticklish stuff," and he wished to be careful.   Just why Scotch congregations should be more " ticklish " in America than in Scotland he probably did not know, but the fact that they are ticklish was to him so important a truth that he underlined the statement in his diary.

On the evening of April 18th, 1859, the congregation did formally what they had months before practically decided to do—they called Mr. Cochrane.   The call was soon afterwards sustained and accepted, and on the 23rd day of May the Presbytery met to examine him for ordination. The examination seems to have been thorough, but it was successfully passed, and on the 7th day of June the ordination and induction took place. The services were impressive, and the people gave their young pastor an enthusiastic reception. Mr. Cochrane thus describes his own feelings : " The exercises were solemn throughout, especially when I kneeled to receive the ordination by the laying on of their hands. I never felt so unworthy and so sinful, and I hope that this feeling may not be evanescent. Oh, what a miserable, poor, unworthy sinner to occupy such a solemn position ! May God give me grace to walk humbly, and henceforth to know nothing but Christ and Him crucified."

The youthful pastor of the Scotch church had little to learn about congregational work. He had a fine natural turn for ecclesiastical affairs. In Paisley he had taken an active part in the work of the Free Middle Church. In Cincinnati, Hanover and Princeton he had kept himself in touch with congregational life. Natural aptitude and experience made it comparatively easy for him to start in Jersey City without making the mistakes that are so easily made in a first pastorate. He knew his field pretty well, for he had preached to the congregation frequently and had done some pastoral work among the sick during his weekly visits to the city. The morning after his induction he started work, not only with enthusiasm, but with that knowledge and experience which never fail to make enthusiasm useful.

For some time he lived with a relative in New York, named Mr. William Wilson. Mr. Wilson's kindness knew no bounds. He fitted up and furnished a room in his house as a study, and in many other ways helped Mr. Cochrane to make a good start in clerical life. And a good start he certainly did make. He prepared his sermons carefully, and usually spent the afternoons and many of the evenings in earnest pastoral work. At his first communion season twenty-seven new members were added to the roll. The people were quickened, and the heart of the young pastor gladdened.

All, however, was not gladness. Then, and during the whole of his after life, Dr. Cochrane made a habit of dealing personally with people that he thought should be members of the Church in full communion. There was one man in the congregation that the young pastor believed was a disciple secretly, though he had never professed his faith in Christ. He spoke to the man several times in private, but all his efforts were in vain. The failure deeply grieved him. " Talked again to Mr. ——— on the subject of the communion. Still he refuses, and why I know not. It grieves me to find him so obstinate. I can do no more but pray that God's Spirit may touch his heart. Oh, it is trying to my sensitive nature to meet with such rebuffs thus early." The young pastor had found the limit of his power early in his ministry. His experience was by no means exceptional. Any earnest minister soon finds the limit of his power in dealing with men.

About a month after his induction a little incident occurred which showed that Mr. Cochrane was substantially the same man at the beginning of his ministry as he was all the way through. Let him relate the incident himself: "I want our church trustees to furnish the vacant room in the basement for their own and my comfort, and to run a stair up to the church, which would enable me to enter the pulpit without coming up the aisle. They are, however, very dilatory about a small matter. I told them I would rather raise the money for it myself than have any ado about it." True to the life. To the end of his days when things ought to be done, if other people would not do them, the Doctor did them himself.

At this period in his life Mr. Cochrane was easily hurt by what he called "rebuffs," but he was easily encouraged, and much of his experience was of a

very encouraging nature. One Sabbath, a few weeks
after his induction, he preached for a friend in Dobbs
Ferry. Dr. Gardiner Spring, of the Murray Hill
church, happened to be one of his hearers. At the
close of the service, " Dr. Spring," he says, "came to
me, shook hands very warmly, thanked me for my sermon, and gave me some words of affectionate counsel.
It gratified me very much to have such an expression of feeling from such a man." May a kind
heaven send hearers like Gardiner Spring to all our
churches.

At the close of a year of earnest and successful
work we find Mr. Cochrane on board the steamship
Africa, accompanied by his friends, Mr. and Mrs.
Wilson, bound for Paisley. The voyage was, on the
whole, pleasant. Though he suffered a few days from
sea-sickness, he had no such experiences as were his
six years before on his voyage to New York. He
became acquainted with one or two clergymen, and
had "long talks with the head engineer," probably
getting from that important officer some illustrations
to be used in the making of sermons in Jersey City.
One couple on board, perhaps, furnished him with
material which may have lighted up a paragraph in
some future speech or lecture. " We had an English
lady on board that has utterly disgusted me. Her
husband is some twenty years older than herself.

They have two children, which the old man has to trot around wearily from early morn till late at night whilst 'my Ladye' sits at her ease scolding, talking, fretting, grumbling, eating and drinking. If I had such a woman I should apply for a divorce to-morrow."

On the morning of July 2nd the *Africa* arrived in Liverpool. There Mr. Cochrane met his old friend, Mr. McKinlay, from Paisley. They spent the day together, and in the evening Mr. Cochrane sailed for Greenock on the *Princess Royal*. At four o'clock next afternoon he arrived in Paisley, and at five saw the friend he had crossed the Atlantic to bring to Jersey City. Whether his business was ecclesiastical or matrimonial, Dr. Cochrane never allowed the grass to grow under his feet.

Needless to say he got a warm welcome from his old friends in Paisley, and from none a more cordial greeting than from his former pastor, Mr. Fraser. The next three weeks were spent in visiting old friends, and busy, happy weeks they were. He preached every Sabbath, and, of course, his old companions were all out to hear him. Every minister knows how his schoolmates, male and female, stand by him when he makes his first appearance in the pulpit in his native place.

On the 24th of July Mr. Cochrane and Miss Mary

Houston, of Paisley, were united in marriage. The ceremony was performed by Mr. Hutton, the bride's pastor, and Mr. Fraser offered the opening prayer. A few days were spent in Edinburgh, and the happy couple returned to Paisley. Nearly a month was spent in visiting friends in and around Paisley, and the day soon came when they must start for America and begin life's battle in earnest. Among the many friends they met at this time were Dr. and Mrs. Burns, who gave the young minister and his bride a hearty invitation to visit them in Toronto. A farewell *soirée* was given in Mr. Fraser's church, which was attended by many representative people. Farewell speeches were delivered by Mr. Fraser and others. Mr. Cochrane usually kept his wits about him on such occasions, but his own criticism on his reply was, " I don't know what I said."

After many farewells the young couple left for Liverpool on the evening of August 23rd. Mr. Fraser's last words were, " William, you won't be long in America." Happily for the Home Mission interests of the Presbyterian Church in Canada, the good man's prediction did not prove true. At midnight Mr. Cochrane ran up against his friend and neighbour, Dr. Thomson, of New York, on the platform of the railway station at Carlisle. Strange how people do sometimes meet in this world!

The following day was spent by Mr. Cochrane and Mr. Wilson in getting their luggage on board the steamer. After the lionizing and feasting in Paisley this sort of work seemed rather prosaic; but it had to be done.

At noon on the 25th, Mr. and Mrs. Cochrane and Mr. and Mrs. Wilson went on board the steamship *America* and set sail for Boston *via* Halifax. The weather for a considerable part of the voyage was rough, and for the ten thousandth time it was made painfully clear that sea-sickness is no respecter of persons. Even young clergymen and their brides are not exempt.

At five o'clock on the evening of September 6th the *America* landed at her dock in the harbour of Halifax. As the vessel had to remain for four hours, Mr. Cochrane "walked up through the town." To put the matter mildly, his first impressions of the town were not specially favourable. Little did the young minister think that evening, as he walked about in the old capital a total stranger, that in the coming years he should act a prominent part in two General Assemblies in that same city, and have many warm friends and admirers there.

The journey from Halifax to Jersey City was soon over, and the young pastor and his bride got a warm welcome from his congregation. A public reception was given in the basement of the church, and the ladies of the congregation presented Mrs. Cochrane with one hundred dollars.

True to his nature, the first three days he was on the ground Mr. Cochrane visited all the sick in the congregation, and all the families death had entered during his absence.   He had large audiences the first Sabbath he preached, and his second start in Jersey City was a pronounced success.

Privileges, however, always bring responsibilities, as the following entries in his diary during the second week clearly show : " Searching all day for a house, but found none.   Don't know what to do in the matter."   " To-day at Jersey City continuing my fruitless search for a house.   Cale's house decidedly the best ; but the wherewithal to buy *non est.*"   " No study all this week, and Friday night come !!"   Men or women who have " searched " for a suitable house in a large city will understand the meaning of these entries quite as sympathetically as they will understand anything in this biography.

The Scotch congregation was small in numbers when Mr. Cochrane became its pastor, but under his vigorous ministrations it grew steadily in numbers and efficiency.   Soon after his return from Paisley a movement was made in the direction of securing a new church building.   The effort was successful, and in 1861 a church on Grove Street was purchased from the Unitarians, and the congregation moved into their new church home. The pastor became more and more known as a vigorous evangelical preacher, and the congregation grew in numbers, spirituality, and working power. Thus the good work went on until, in December, 1861, Mr. Cochrane visited his friend, Dr. Thompson, who had removed to Galt, Ont., and the people of Zion Church, Brantford, coveted the pastor of Grove Street Presbyterian Church, Jersey City. There was, naturally enough, some "dryness" on the part of the people when their pastor accepted the call to Zion Church, but it soon passed away, and they became in after years the best of friends.

Several things should be noted about Mr. Cochrane's pastorate in Jersey City. The congregation grew, and the young pastor grew as well. It was a growing time for both. There were many advantages in living so near a great city like New York, and Mr. Cochrane was just the young man to make the most of these advantages. Some of the New York and Brooklyn pulpits were filled by men of power, and he never missed an opportunity to hear them. The storm that burst in the long civil war was gathering. Henry Ward Beecher was doing his greatest work on the platform and in the pulpit. The young pastor came under the power of his mighty eloquence, and the power was felt for many a year. He had no sympathy with Beecher's theology, and no admiration for what he used to call " Beecherisms," but he thought Beecher was easily the first orator in America, if not in the world. Books and all kinds of current literature were easily obtained in New York, and Mr. Cochrane was a generous, perhaps we should say an omnivorous, reader. Carter's bookstore was his favourite resort. Many happy friendships were made in the great city, and most of them lasted throughout life. One of the most sympathetic and appreciative articles on Dr. Cochrane's life and work appeared in the *Scottish American* a few days after his death. No confidence is violated by saying that the article was from the pen of his life-long friend, Dr. A. M. Stewart, editor of that excellent journal.

CHAPTER IV.

Call to Zion Church, Brantford—Induction—State of the congregation—Its growth—Labours in other places—Pulpit Preparation—Pastoral work—Resolution of Presbytery of Paris.

DR. JOHN THOMSON, of New York, happened to be present at an oral examination in Dr. McGill's class-room in Princeton, in April, 1858. At the close of the examination he introduced himself to one of the students as a "brother Scotchman," spoke very kindly to him, and asked the young man to visit him in New York the following week. The student's name was William Cochrane, and this little incident in Dr. McGill's class-room was the pivot on which turned Mr. Cochrane's life in Canada. He visited Dr. Thomson, and the Doctor took quite a friendly interest in him afterwards. When Mr. Cochrane became pastor of the Scotch church in Jersey City, he and Dr. Thomson were quite neighbourly and often exchanged work. Nothing was more natural than a visit by Mr. Cochrane to Dr. Thomson in Galt when Dr. Thomson became pastor of Knox Church in that

Canadian town.   The visit was made in December, 1861.   During Mr. Cochrane's stay in Galt, Dr. Thomson was invited to speak at a social meeting which the people of Zion Church, Brantford, were to hold on the twentieth day of December, in Kerby Hall. Dr. Thomson took his visitor with him, and the visitor made one of those rattling speeches for which he was noted.   It was a clear case of love at first sight.   Mr. Cochrane preached one Sabbath, was called a few weeks afterwards, and inducted on the 14th day of May, 1862.   The call was signed by 153 members and 56 adherents.

Had Dr. Thomson not spoken to the student that day in Dr. McGill's class-room, Mr. Cochrane, in all probability, would never have worked a day in Canada.   On what a seemingly small matter one's life-work may turn.   It would be interesting to know what it was that led Dr. Thomson to notice that particular student among so many others.   Possibly it was his dialect, for the Doctor introduced himself as a "brother Scotchman."   Perhaps his clever answers may have attracted attention, for Mr. Cochrane writes that he "got along very well" in that examination— a verdict which he passed on very few of his examinations.   Whatever it was that attracted the kind Doctor's attention, that friendly little interview was the first link in a chain of circumstances that brought Mr.

Cochrane to Canada and gave the Presbyterianism of Canada his great services.

Zion Church, Brantford, at the time Mr. Cochrane first knew it, was not what, in Presbyterian parlance, is called a "desirable vacancy." According to the "retrospect" published in the last annual report of the congregation, written by the careful pen of Sheriff Watt, the number of members in 1862 was about 150. The congregation was small, but the debt was large. In a "boom" time a small number of enthusiastic, enterprising Free Church men built a new church, which cost $17,000. Had the inflation been real and lasting prosperity, the little congregation could have got on well enough, for the men who led in the enterprise were of the best class. But the inevitable depression came. A financial storm swept over the Province, "crippling some and ruining many others." The "boom" burst, but the mortgages remained, as they always do. Zion Church had a debt of about $9,000, and the interest had to be met out of a revenue contributed by one hundred and fifty people, some of them financially weakened by the collapse of the "boom." So serious was the financial situation of the congregation that the Presbytery sent three of its members—one to Hamilton, another to Toronto, and a third to Montreal—to solicit aid; but their mission met with only moderate success. The Rev. Andrew

ZION PRESBYTERIAN CHURCH, BRANTFORD.

Tolmie, of Southampton, is the only one of the three now alive. Mr. Cochrane must have known all about the financial condition of the congregation when he was called. He was a capital business man, and no doubt he examined the situation carefully. Nothing that he ever did showed his undoubted courage to greater advantage than it was shown when he took hold of this struggling little body of people, burdened with debt, deserted by their former pastor, and resolved to sink or swim with them.

The induction took place on the 14th day of May, 1862. The Rev. Walter Inglis, of Ayr, presided; Mr. Geo. Irving, of the same place, preached from Haggai ii. 7; Mr. Cross, of Ingersoll, addressed the minister, and Mr. McMullen the people. Thirteen ministers were present and much interest was manifested in the proceedings. Of those who took part in the induction services Dr. McMullen is the only one now remaining.

The report, from which we have already quoted, says :

"Mr. Cochrane proceeded to the work of building up the congregation with energy and enthusiasm. In 1863 the membership had increased to 260; the total income to $2,450, of which some $600 had to be devoted to interest on the debt. In 1864 mission schools in connection with the church were organized in the East Ward and West Brantford, and a year later in Eagle Place, all of which were very successful, those in the East Ward and Eagle Place being discontinued when other churches were built in the localities. West Brantford mission still flourishes, and also 'St. Andrew's,' started some eight years ago, both of which now possess neat and commodious edifices.

"In 1867, to meet the increasing demand for accommodation, galleries were built and the building generally renovated and improved. In 1871 the balance of the church debt, some $5,000, was wiped out by special subscription and the minister's stipend raised to $1,600. In 1876 a new organ was added, to make room for which another enlargement had to be made, and thereafter there was a marked improvement in the service of praise. The capacity of the church soon, however, became too small for the requirements, and another large addition was found necessary. Some $15,000 were expended in enlarging, remodelling, and frescoing, in heightening and slating the spire, and in furnishing. The seating capacity was thus increased to 1,000; also furnishing additional rooms in the basement for the use of Bible classes, vestry, etc. The ladies undertook the carpeting and cushioning of the auditorium, which was carried out in a handsome and substantial manner. The church was re-opened April 8th, 1883.

"Throughout the whole of Dr. Cochrane's ministry the growth of the congregation in numbers and strength was steady and substantial. The church in 1862 numbered 150, and contributed about $2,000 for church purposes, including $800 for stipend; while in 1898 there were 830 members, contributing $8,205 for church purposes, including stipend, $2,400."

It is only fair to say that the conditions under which Dr. Cochrane laboured in Brantford were, on the whole, highly favourable as compared with the conditions under which many of his brethren are compelled to labour. During the thirty-six years of his pastorate the population grew from 6,000 to 18,000. Brantford was a good place to work in, and he had some good men to work with. Dr. Cochrane has often been described as a "unique personality." There must have been several other rare personalities in Zion Church during his ministry if we may judge by the length of their services in the congregation. In this age of fickleness and change it is refreshing to read the following extract from the last annual report of Zion Church:

"As the church has had but two pastors, so it has had but two chairmen of management and two session clerks. The late James Wallace was chairman from the inception down to 1875, was treasurer for fifteen years of this period, and elder down to his death, in 1885 ; for over ten years occupying the triple position of chairman, treasurer and elder.   William Watt, the present chairman, has held the place for twenty-five years, and has been a manager for thirty-five. George Watt has been a manager for the whole period of the church's existence, nearly forty-five years. Adam Spence and Thos. McLean have been in office either as manager or elder for the same period. Wm. Grant has been treasurer for a quarter of a century. The late John Sutherland was manager, elder and secretary for many years. Dr. Nichol has long been an active worker as superintendent of the Sabbath School, and as director of Bible classes and services in the missions. The first session clerk was Mr. A. I. MacKenzie, who returned to Hamilton in 1855. Mr. (now Rev.) Andrew Hudson was then appointed, retiring in 1870, and was succeeded by Thos. McLean, the present incumbent. Others might be mentioned who have long been actively identified with the schemes of Zion Church and its missions, did space permit."

If, as is sometimes alleged, the Presbyterianism of Canada is losing its historic steadiness and solidity, the decline has manifestly not struck Zion Church, Brantford.

Mr. Cochrane's services were not long confined to

his own congregation. His neighbours soon discovered that there was a live man in the pulpit of
Zion Church, and they called on him for work, as they
usually do in such cases. Always willing to help, for
he was the most unselfish and obliging of neighbours,
he soon made the circuit of his own Presbytery.
The people like to see an exhibition of life, and the
new minister from Brantford put any amount of life
into all his work. Whether he preached, or lectured,
or delivered a missionary address, or spoke at a *soirée*,
he always stirred things up. Whatever else he was
or was not, he was never dull. Somebody has said
that dullness is the unpardonable sin in preaching and
public speaking. Mr. Cochrane may or may not have
thought so, but he certainly did avoid dullness in his
public appearances. Truth to say, the effort did not
cost him much. Nature had made him a lively man
—stupidity was quite beyond his reach.

The influence of the rising pastor of Zion Church
soon extended beyond his own Presbytery. During
the first ten years of his pastorate he visited many
parts of Ontario and lectured or preached in the
interests of Presbyterianism. Lecturing was popular
in those days, and he did good work on the lecture
platform. His old lecture on the "Hero Martyrs of
Scotland" stirred the blood, and stiffened the back,
and moistened the eyes of many a Presbyterian. No

man with a drop of the "true blue" in his veins ever heard that lecture without feeling proud of the history of his Church.

He was much in demand for church openings, anniversaries, missionary meetings, and his speech was the chief feature of many a good old-fashioned *soirée*. The annual congregational *soirée* was at its best in those days. The best ministers in the Church spoke at meetings of that kind, and Mr. Cochrane did his full share, and perhaps a little more.

A glance over the list of places in which the pastor of Zion Church rendered service brings out one striking feature of his character. His work was not confined to the larger, and what are sometimes erroneously called the more important, congregations of the Church. He went, if he could go, wherever a struggling minister needed him. He had known something of hardship himself in his early days, and the brother minister whose back was to the wall never appealed to him in vain. Mr. Cochrane liked a large audience and a popular occasion as well as most other ministers like such things, but he did not take a week to consider whether any place to which he was invited was important enough for him to preach the Gospel in. He was willing to go wherever he was needed and wanted, and he went if he could. He increased the attendance at many a meeting by addressing it, and that is more than some of us can do.

Early in 1871 death entered Mr. Cochrane's home. On the morning of Sabbath, January 7th, as the church bells were ringing, Mrs. Cochrane was called to the Church above. She had been in failing health for some time, but the end came with alarming suddenness. He had prepared two sermons, hoping to preach as usual ; but on Sabbath morning it became painfully evident that the duty of that day was to wait and suffer. At ten minutes to eleven the final call came.

When Mr. Cochrane left Paisley for America, in 1854, there was an understanding between him and Miss Mary Houston that she should become Mrs. Cochrane when he became a minister. During all his student life in America she had corresponded with him. He brought her to his first home in Jersey City. She had helped him during the years that he was making his place in the Canadian Church. Now he is suddenly left alone with two motherless children. Kind friends did all in their power to help him in his bereavement, but there are wounds which the best of friends cannot heal.

In a trouble like that which now darkened Mr. Cochrane's home some men give up public work in so far as they can and suffer in the seclusion of their homes. Others plunge more deeply into work, and try by increased activity to keep themselves from brooding over their loss. Mr. Cochrane pursued the latter, and, for a man of his disposition, no doubt wiser, course. He cancelled some engagements, but by the end of the year was more immersed in work than ever before.

Soon after his bereavement he made what seems to have been the mistake of his life by allowing himself to be overloaded with work. In 1872 he accepted the Convenership of the Home Mission Committee, and that added greatly to his work and responsibility. The Muskoka region was being opened up for settlement, and there was much mission work to be done in that part of Ontario. Manitoba and the North-West Territories had just became part of the Dominion, and the Church had to follow the settlers in the "great lone land." It was fortunate for the Presbyterianism of Canada that such men as Cochrane, King, Warden, Laing, and others were at the helm at this juncture. As Mr. Cochrane's part in the work will be dealt with in another chapter, it is not necessary to say more here than that his burdens were now greatly increased.

In 1874 he, along with other enterprising citizens of Brantford, founded the Brantford Young Ladies' College. Mr. Cochrane's influence and popularity were part, and no small part either, of the working capital of the institution. He and his fellow labourers had not gone far when they found out that managing a ladies' college is, to put the matter mildly, not all pleasure.

In 1875, immediately after the Union, he was appointed Clerk of the Synod of Hamilton and London. He had for years been Clerk of the Presbytery of Paris, and though an expert at writing minutes, he found the two clerkships burdensome.

In addition to his Church work he was President of the Mechanics Institute, and selected and purchased personally much of the literature for the Free Library of the city.

Over and above the work that devolved upon him officially, there were many other duties that came his way as an active member of the community. Mr. Cochrane never was born to take a back seat in anything. He instinctively took a hand in everything, and often got the heavy end of the work to do.

The pastorate of Zion Church, pulpit and platform work in all parts of the province, with occasional visits to Montreal, Manitoba, and different cities in the United States, the Presidency of a Ladies' College, with classes to teach and many other duties and responsibilities in connection with the institution, the Convenership of the Home Mission Committee, and the Clerkship of two Courts, made more work and worry than any man could stand with safety—not to speak of reasonable comfort—even though the man

6

was the Rev. William Cochrane. There is a limit to human endurance, however willing a man may be to work or suffer. Overdrafts on the body and mind come due with as much certainty as drafts on the bank, and Mr. Cochrane's overdrafts began to come in about 1878 and 1879. In 1878 there are many intimations in his diary that the burden was too heavy, though he did not put it in that way. In the following year he had to stop work and go to Europe for three months.

In order to convey something like a correct idea of Mr. Cochrane's activity, we may take specimen weeks from the record made by himself. Here is the record of a week from home, the first Sabbath being spent in his own church: "Preached on Joshua iii. 4 and Luke xiii. 5—Attended Sabbath Schools—Monday at Council meeting—Tuesday at Presbytery of Stratford and Mayor's dinner—Wednesday, Orillia—Thursday, Beaverton—Friday, Port Hope—Saturday, Sabbath, and Monday, Deseronto—Tuesday, back to Brantford." That is a fair record for one week in midwinter, but it is eclipsed by the following record, made in six days at home about the same time: "At Presbytery on Tuesday—Wrote two sermons—Visited all the sick—Attended three funerals (names given, one of the funerals being in Mount Pleasant)—At prayer-meeting and teachers' meeting—Spoke at Cameron's farewell meeting—Wrote about 20 letters

—Had another attack of blindness and sickness— Corrected proofs of my book daily—Began Home Mission Report for General Assembly—Preached from Philippians iii. 20, 21 and Rev. ii. 17—Visited Sabbath Schools."

Writing two sermons in five days and preaching them on the sixth, especially when one of the texts is Rev. ii. 17, is fair work, but the pastor of Zion Church would probably have thought that the writing of the sermons and preaching them did not give him more than useful exercise.

The record of these weeks, taken almost at random from his diary, is a fair specimen of Mr. Cochrane's working weeks during the last twenty-five years of his life in Brantford. Of course the work varied. At times he gave his time and strength chiefly to pastoral work, and visited incessantly until he got over all the districts into which the congregation was divided From March until the end of June the Home Mission Committee, the Synod, and the General Assembly claimed special attention. Immediately after the meeting of the General Assembly, sometimes before the meeting was over, he had to rush home to the closing exercises of the Ladies' College. Whatever the nature of the work, there was always plenty of it —sometimes far too much. The only thing that decreased was Mr. Cochrane's strength. He knew quite well that he was overworked, and made several attempts to lessen his labours, but the attempts were not all successful. In 1877 he resigned the Convenership of the Home Mission Committee, but the General Assembly did not accept the resignation. At different times he gave up, in whole or in part, his work in the college, but he always went back again, and was Governor of the institution when he died. In 1878 he resigned the Clerkship of the Paris Presbytery, and that was, perhaps, the only work he really stopped doing during the whole of his life in Brantford.

The fact is, it was not Mr. Cochrane's disposition to give up any kind of work in which he was engaged. He might feel the pressure and talk about stopping, but when the time to stop came he did not like to do it, and if he did stop he was very likely to start again. Proof reading was to him one of the most irksome of all duties, and he never had more delightful moments than when he got the last proof sheets of a book into the printer's hands. Anybody who saw him at that time would conclude that his last volume was in the press. It might not be so. Any day, when he felt fairly well, he might undertake to publish another. Dr. Cochrane could advance against any odds; but he never could retreat, or even stand at ease.

It is easy to understand that people who appointed

Dr. Cochrane to do any work never wanted him to stop. He was prompt, accurate, thorough—above everything, thorough—in all he did. Slipshod was with him the unpardonable sin in work. He never thought anything was done until it was done right. Ministers are not, as a rule, the best men of business, and when they secure the services of a thorough business man like Dr. Cochrane, or Dr. Torrance, or Dr. Warden, they always use him as long as he is willing to be used, and sometimes longer.

On the 2nd day of October, 1873, Mr. Cochrane was united in marriage to Miss Balmer, of Oakville, eldest daughter of the late Mr. Robert Balmer, who for nearly half a century held the position of postmaster in that town. Mr. Balmer was a man of sterling worth, quiet and unassuming in manner, but firm in principle, and strongly attached to the doctrine and polity of his Church. He served in the eldership for more than fifty years. He and Mrs. Balmer were active members of the Presbyterian congregation of Oakville almost from its organization, and Miss Balmer had been trained from infancy to take an interest in Church work. Brought up by such parents and in such surroundings, she had little, if anything, to learn about Church affairs when she became Mrs. Cochrane. The troops of friends who— some of them many times—enjoyed her hospitality in Brantford, know well that she had nothing to learn about domestic arrangements. How faithfully she helped her husband during twenty-five years of strenuous labour, and in some severe trials, is known only to him who is gone and to the Master he served.

In 1875 the Senate of Hanover College conferred the degree of Doctor in Divinity upon the pastor of Zion Church, and in the remaining pages of this volume he must be called Dr. Cochrane.

In 1882 the General Assembly unanimously elected him Moderator. Twenty years of faithful service in the Church, and ten years special service as Convener of the Home Mission Committee, brought him the highest position in the Supreme Court. The honor has not always been so fairly earned.

The main secret of Dr. Cochrane's success as a minister was that he ardently loved his work. Almost from infancy he longed to be a minister. The dream of his boyhood was to preach the Gospel. When a clerk in Paisley, and a student in Hanover, if sermons he heard did not seem to have the necessary amount of " pith " he always resolved to preach with energy if he ever got a pulpit. The resolution was well kept. If he heard sermons that he thought had not enough of Christ in them, and that did not deal closely with unsaved men, he earnestly prayed that if he ever became a preacher he might have strength given him to preach Christ fully and faithfully to dying men. The prayer was answered. He loved to preach, and he spared no pains in the preparation of his sermons. His usual method was to write both sermons in full if he possibly could. Of course, that was often impossible during the last twenty-five years of his life, but he always kept the written sermon before his mind as his ideal. He could preach as well as most men from a " skeleton," but he never liked skeletons. When Dr. Storr's little book appeared, Dr. Cochrane became a convert, and he used to go into the pulpit without a scrap of paper of any kind. The carefully prepared sermon was left on his desk. He was enthusiastic about the Storrs method for some time, but he gradually got back to the old plan of having a few notes before him, whether he used them or not. When Dr. Cochrane finished writing a sermon it was ready for the press. The thoroughness with which he did everything is nowhere more strikingly seen than in the pile of manuscripts he left behind him. He wrote a clear, bold, characteristic hand, punctuated and paragraphed in a way that would gladden the heart of the most finical compositor, and from the first word to the last there was not a blot nor an erasure. Three days before his death, when the last enemy was knocking at the door, he wrote one of the handsomest manuscript sermons that he left behind him, and that is saying much.

Dr. Cochrane was in the highest sense of the term an evangelical preacher. The texts he preached on during his whole life are in his diary, and they clearly show that the main object of his pulpit work was to bring sinners to Christ, and to edify, strengthen and comfort believers. An occasional sermon on some current topic only tends to accentuate the main drift of his pulpit work. He never made the fatal error of assuming that all his hearers were converted, nor did he ever teach men that sin was nothing more than their misfortune. The old theology, as he heard it in Paisley and was taught it in Princeton, he preached to the end of his days in Zion Church, and never with more emphasis and pathos than during the closing years of his ministry.

Dr. Cochrane knew very well that many of his duties did not help to increase his power in the pulpit. He lived in constant fear that engrossing minutes, drawing up reports, writing " multitudes of letters on all sorts of subjects, to all sorts of people," might secularize his mind. There is something pathetic in the frequency with which he expresses this fear in his diary. " No time for solid study, no time for meditation ; *but what can I do ?* " Occasionally, their gloom, and produce a joy before unknown. Verily Verily I say unto you, that ye shall weep and lament, and ye shall be sorrow-ful, but your sorrow shall be turned into joy. Ye now therefore have sorrow, but I will see you again, and your heart shall rejoice, and your joy no man taketh from you". And so shall it be with suffering saints when Jesus comes again.

> "No more heart-pangs or sadness
>   When Jesus comes;
> All peace, and joy, and gladness
>   When Jesus Comes.
> All doubts and fears will vanish
>   When Jesus Comes.
> All gloom his face will banish,
>   When Jesus Comes

Life at the longest is but brief, and our sorrow cannot survive it. In that bright world, whither we are hasting, all cause for melancholy is removed. There are no tears to dim the Vision of the redeemed. The last sigh—the last pang, the last

when driven with Church business of one kind and another, he would ask himself, " Is this the right kind of work for a Gospel minister ? " Once he almost bitterly complained that he had to be doing business when he ought to be " dealing with souls." Another day he writes : " My work is getting to be as much secular as religious."

It was well for Dr. Cochrane and for Zion Church that the fear of having his mind secularized did constantly follow him. His sense of danger prompted him to use proper means to ward off the threatened evil. He read devotional books for the express purpose of keeping his mind and heart in the proper condition for preaching and dealing with parishioners about spiritual matters. He studied the biographies of eminent ministers who had led busy lives. The life of Dr. James Hamilton he found specially useful.

The one thing above all others, however, that kept Dr. Cochrane from being a business man, and nothing more, was his constant contact with suffering humanity. He was at his best when visiting the sick and praying with dying parishioners. Those who merely saw Dr. Cochrane on the platform, or in the Church Courts, or committee-room, or even in the pulpit, never knew the man. His best work was done in the house of mourning. He was tender hearted and sympathetic, and spared no labour or pains in helping parishioners under any kind of a cloud. When a home was darkened by death, or something worse than death had crimsoned the cheeks of a family, the pastor was the first to come, if he knew, and the last to leave.

Like all strong, aggressive men, Dr. Cochrane was willing enough to have his own way at times in church matters. A member of Zion Church was once asked why he did not speak out and oppose something or another that the Doctor wanted done. "I often made up my mind to do so," said the good man, "but when I think of the number of times he came at midnight to pray with my dying girl, I am dumb." Dr. Cochrane was a good preacher, but it was not his preaching alone that gave him his wonderful hold on Zion Church. He gave many a good speech and delivered some excellent lectures ; but some pastors just as brilliant on the platform as he was have had short pastorates. He was a capital organizer, but organization is not everything. Some congregations are organized to death. Dr. Cochrane's strong hold on Zion Church may be attributed mainly to his constant, sympathetic, helpful, self-denying work among the poor, the troubled, the sick, and the dying. The general public may scarcely believe this. The general public does not know the facts as well as they are known to one who has studied the daily life of Dr. Cochrane, written by himself.

The question has many a time been asked, " How can a man so busy with Church affairs as Dr. Cochrane always was attend to his pastoral work ? " Dr. Cochrane was not an ordinary man, and cannot be judged by ordinary rules. Most ministers take a much needed rest after coming home from the Church courts, or from a preaching or lecturing tour. Dr. Cochrane often left his valise at his house and then visited half a dozen sick people, and attended to any other pastoral duties that were waiting for him. In an emergency, or rather in what he in his solicitude considered an emergency, he would go straight from the railway station and work among his people as if he had come fresh from his home. At the end of a long day's work in the Church courts, or on his return from a lecturing tour, or long journey, he could put on his study gown and begin a sermon or answer a bundle of letters, and do it all in a natural matter-of-course kind of way impossible to ordinary men. Of course it was all done at the expense of his health, to say nothing about his comfort ; but, all the same, it was done.

There was no year in the thirty-six—except, perhaps, the last one—in which Dr. Cochrane did not visit pastorally all the families in Zion Church. The congregation was well organized, and he could make a great many visits in a week if other matters did not interfere. The highest number we find recorded for one week is forty, but he often made fifteen or twenty, and did not seem to think that there was anything unusual about twenty visits when he was giving special attention to that kind of work.

Dr. Cochrane's promptitude and punctuality helped him greatly in his pastoral work. He never sauntered about among his parishioners. He knew just where he wanted to go, and what he wanted to do, and he went straight to the place and did it. He never kept anybody waiting for him, and if anybody kept him waiting, his usual amiability was perhaps a little disturbed. Dr. Cochrane could give away money freely enough, but it did worry him to lose time. He never spent a moment looking for things. He could lay his hand on any book or paper in his study without the loss of a second. He could make a pastoral call while a minister of the opposite type was finding his hat.

Besides his regular pastoral visitation and visitation of the sick and troubled, Dr. Cochrane made special visits to adherents that he thought should be members in full communion. He began this kind of work in Jersey City, and continued it throughout the whole of his ministry. Before each communion season, afternoons and evenings were spent in dealing personally with people that he thought were almost persuaded and not far from the kingdom. He never allowed his relations with any man to become such that he could not speak to him about his spiritual concerns. Dr. Cochrane was a social man, and he enjoyed social life. He was a citizen, and identified himself with many public affairs. He spoke at public dinners and attended all kinds of public meetings; but he never forgot that he was a minister of Christ. Whether his gift for personal dealing with men in regard to their spiritual interests was natural or acquired, or partly both, he had it in large measure, and made full use of it during the whole of his ministry. Happy is the pastor who can speak wisely to individual men about their personal salvation.

In going in and out among his people, Dr. Cochrane resorted to no unworthy means to make himself popular. He wore no professional smile. He never pretended to have more interest in his parishioners than he really felt. He was not a "yes, yes" man, who agreed with everything that everybody said. In fact, he was quite as ready to argue with a man as agree with him if he thought duty required argument. He never played the demagogue nor wore unclerical clothes in order to please certain kinds of people. Everywhere and always he was a dignified and well-dressed minister who respected his calling. The people well knew he was their friend, and no fishing for popularity was needed.

Dr. and Mrs. Cochrane were given to hospitality—in fact, they were very much given to it. One who had good reason to know described their home as the "Cochrane Hotel." It may not be good taste, even in a biography, to turn a good man's house inside out and ask the public to look at the number of people he and his good lady entertain. Suffice it to say, the Cochrane family hardly ever lived alone, and there were many times when it puzzled one to see where they found a corner in their own home to live in at all.

Zion Church dealt generously with Dr. Cochrane in the matter of vacations. He crossed the Atlantic fifteen times, twelve times during his pastorate in Brantford. Sometimes the people gave him a generous purse when he was leaving, and always gave him a hearty welcome when he returned.

In 1869 he crossed the ocean with Mrs. Cochrane, visited Paisley and other places in Scotland, representing the Canadian Church in the Scottish Assemblies. Ten years later he visited Great Britain again, and was away three months. In 1884 he had another vacation of three months, and visited Scotland, Ireland, England, Belgium, Germany, Switzerland and France. In 1888 he crossed the Atlantic again and made a long continental tour with the late Dr. Waters, visiting many places of interest. In 1894, accompanied by his daughter, he spent two months in Great Britain and France. His last long vacation was taken in 1896, when he and Mrs. Cochrane spent three months in Europe. Many shorter tours, partly on duty and partly for pleasure, were thrown in between these longer vacations. His love for New York and its vicinity continued to the end of his life, and he often paid a flying visit to the great city, preached or spoke at some meeting of Scotchmen, and called on his old friends. Whatever may have been Dr. Cochrane's failings—and, like all mortals, he had his failings and limitations—he never forgot the friends of his youth. He always alluded to Robert Brown as "my best earthly friend outside of my own home," and nothing pleased him so much as to go back to Cincinnati, Madison and Hanover, and visit the friends of his college days. His last visit was made in the autumn of 1893, when attending the Chicago Fair. It is thus described by himself:

"Spent a day at the Fair, and then on to Cincinnati on Thursday; to Madison Friday, and Hanover Saturday. Preached at 11 a.m. and 7 p.m. in Madison, and at 3 p.m. in Hanover. Saw old friends and the old college, as well as the new, and silently, in heart, said *farewell.* I shall always love old Hanover."

Then follows a list of the people he called to see, and they are all the people he spent many a pleasant hour with during his student days. Some have become rich, some have become poor, and all have grown old, but Dr. Cochrane had not forgotten one of them.

The weak point about all Dr. Cochrane's vacations was that if he happened to be in any place where the English language was spoken he was very likely to preach three times each Sabbath.

During his pastorate in Brantford he was called five or six times, and was many a time sounded about vacancies, when no further steps were taken, because further steps would have been useless. There is some reason to believe that after his sore bereavement in 1871 he seriously considered an invitation to return to the United States and become pastor of an important congregation. A prominent minister of New York, formerly of Canada, told him that it was now or never. Fortunately for the Presbyterianism of Canada, and perhaps for Dr. Cochrane himself, it turned out to be "never." No doubt he could have done well anywhere, but had he accepted the most tempting call offered, his life might not have been more useful nor his death more regretted.

For one thing not referred to in any of the addresses delivered at his death, he deserves the thanks of all ministers of the Gospel. He proved in the most triumphant manner imaginable that there need be no dead line of fifty, or even of sixty, in the Presbyterian ministry. He died at sixty-eight. The last years of his ministry, judged by the financial and statistical returns, were just as fruitful as any previous year in his long pastorate. Had he given up in time all his work except that done for Zion Church, in all human probability he might have worked on for ten years longer, and the last years might have been among his best.

No good purpose can be served by "padding" out this chapter with details showing the growth of Zion Church from year to year during the thirty-six years of Dr. Cochrane's pastorate. In their essential features the years were much alike. There was substantial progress on the part of the congregation and earnest, self-denying work by the pastor. A glance at the figures quoted in the beginning of this chapter from the last congregational report of Zion Church will show the progress made in so far as such progress can be expressed in figures. The select few who enjoy reading statistics can find the financial and statistical history of Zion Church embedded—perhaps we should say entombed—in thirty-six volumes of the Presbyterian Blue Book. As a record of successful church work from year to year it is interesting, but there is no room for it in this volume.

The writer of these pages has been asked many

7

times how the pastor of Zion Church, ever on the wing, kept up his reading. "Did he get rusty in his Exegetics?" was one of the questions put by a scholarly minister. He never got rusty in his " Exegetics," nor, for that matter, in anything else. It may be admitted that Dr. Cochrane had to speak too much to be sure of always speaking in his best form. In fact, no speaker, whether he speaks much or little, is always at his best. No clock strikes twelve every time. It may also be admitted that much of the writing he had to do was of a kind that is pretty certain, sooner or later, to run down a man's style. But, admitting these things, it cannot be said that Dr. Cochrane's multitudinous engagements were ever allowed to blunt his taste for reading, or seriously impair his scholarship. He knew his Greek Testament well, and could use it with the greatest facility. He taught a class in New Testament Greek in Hanover with marked success, and never lost his taste for that fine line of study. In fact, one of his hobbies was to buy Greek Testaments. He stood well in Dr. Green's classes in Princeton, and, if we rightly remember, he usually examined in Hebrew when students were being licensed by his Presbytery. The writer was licensed by the Presbytery of Paris, and he distinctly remembers that he was more than satisfied with the critical knowledge of Hebrew Dr. Cochrane displayed in asking him questions.

The pastor of Zion Church was perhaps a generous, rather than a Dative-case, reader. He indulged in a little fiction of the best quality. He read the best poets, and was particularly fond of biography. If he had any specialty in reading, it was in the biographical line. He knew better than most men how to buy books. If he knew of any book that was making a strong impression on the public, he always bought it. His rule, however, was to buy the works of high-class men who wrote but few books. He kept his eye steadily on the lists of British publishers, and when a writer of undoubted standing published a volume it was soon afterwards in Dr. Cochrane's library. His knowledge of the book trade enabled him to buy books much more judiciously than most ministers can do.

In the matter of current literature Dr. Cochrane was simply omnivorous. He devoured newspapers and magazines. In his Paisley days his favourite authors were Chalmers, Hugh Miller and, Macaulay. His favourite sermons were perhaps Guthrie's. In later life he feasted on Spurgeon's sermons when he wished to tone up his spiritual nature for pulpit work. As specimens of pulpit oratory that might, or might not, have any Gospel in them, he had a strong liking for Beecher's sermons. While a young pastor in Jersey City he heard Beecher often and the memory of the Brooklyn orator's mighty voice followed him to the end of his days.

This chapter may be appropriately closed with the following resolution passed by the Presbytery of Paris when Dr. Cochrane completed his quarter of a century of service in Zion Church :

" The Rev. William Cochrane, D.D., minister of Zion Church, Brantford, in this Presbytery, having completed twenty-five years of service in that congregation, the Presbytery desire to put on record their gratitude to the great Head of the Church for sparing their brother and giving him grace and strength to labour through such a lengthened period in the pastorate of said congregation, and for the great success with which his pulpit and pastoral labors have been blessed.

" They further bear grateful testimony to the distinguished service which he has rendered during all these years throughout the bounds of this Presbytery, being ever ready to aid the brethren, and always abounding in the work of the Lord.

" More specially do they, with much gratification, refer to his ceaseless activity and untiring labours in the cause of Home Missions, over which he has presided as the honoured Convener of the General Assembly's Committee for so many years.

" The earnest prayer of his brethren is that he may long be spared to his congregation and to the Church at large, and that he may be greatly honoured and blessed in exercising an ever-increasing power for good by means of the press, the platform and the pulpit."

CHAPTER V.

Home Mission work—Appointed Convener of the Home Mission Committee—Work on the three great mission fields : Manitoba, Muskoka, British Columbia — Addresses — Letters—Reports.

DR. COCHRANE was appointed Convener of the Home Mission Committee of the Canada Presbyterian Church in June, 1872. The General Assembly met that year in Knox Church, Hamilton. The Rev. William Fraser, of Bond Head, one of the clerks of the Assembly, was elected Moderator, and Mr. Cochrane was appointed clerk *pro tem*. The Home Mission report was submitted by Mr. Laing, and on his resignation of the convenership Mr. Cochrane was appointed his successor. Prior to that time Mr. Cochrane had been Convener of the Sabbath School Committee. Mr. Thomson, of Sarnia, was put in the position made vacant by changing Mr. Cochrane from the Sabbath School to the Home Mission Committee. All the esteemed brethren whose names have just been written were plain " Mr. " in 1872, though they all became Doctors a few years afterwa ds.

The new Convener was particularly fortunate in the
time at which he began this most important part of
his life-work. Seven years before his appointment a
new scheme for carrying on Home Mission operations
had been adopted after somewhat strenuous opposition. The chief features of the new scheme were
a central committee for administrative purposes and
a central fund for the payment of home missionaries.
Centralization is always unpopular, and opposition to
it rarely fails to be correspondingly popular. It was
urged that the new plan was an interference with the
rights of Presbyteries. These fundamental courts, it
was contended, should work their own mission fields
in their own way. A central committee, armed with
power to carry on work within the bounds of a Pres-
tery, was alleged to be unconstitutional. These
positions, viewed from a purely constitutional stand-
point, may have had some force, but the exigencies
of the Presbyterian Church demanded more work
and more money and more supervision than many
Presbyteries could supply for the mission fields within
their bounds. One illustration will suffice to make
this sufficiently clear. At the time Dr. Cochrane
became Convener, the Presbytery of Manitoba con-
sisted of John Black, William Fletcher, John McNabb
and George Bryce (we write the names as they are
given in the Blue Book for 1872), ministers; and

Angus Polson, Hon. D. Gunn and John Sutherland, elders. Mr. Black was pastor of the Kildonan congregation. Mr. Fletcher had four stations under his care ; Mr. McNabb, four, with occasional services in a fifth, and Mr. Bryce was Senate and Faculty of the Manitoba College, and preacher for the Presbyterians of Winnipeg. Good men and true all these brethren were, but could they, in addition to their own work, have taken charge of all the Home Mission work between Winnipeg and the Rocky Mountains ? Could they have paid the bill ? To ask these questions is to answer them. The Presbyterianism of Manitoba and the North-West Territories, to say nothing about that of Muskoka, New Ontario, and British Columbia, is a triumphant demonstration that the men who contended for a central fund and a central committee were right. No other plan of campaign could have given Presbyterianism the position the Church occupies in the newer parts of the Dominion.

George Brown used to say that men who initiate and carry out reforms in Church and State rarely get credit for their work. Dr. Laing, of Dundas, might add his sympathetic Amen. He has contended for more schemes that were unpopular in their initiatory stages, and which became both popular and useful afterwards, than any half dozen men in the Presbyterian Church in Canada. He had his usual experience when the new scheme for doing Home Mission work was being devised and put into operation. He was one of the originators, if not the only originator, of the new plan. He worked hard for it in the initiatory stages, and took a prominent part in perfecting the details in the Synod of 1865. Some of the opponents of the new method of working predicted that the scheme would fail, and though they, as loyal Presbyterians, would do nothing in the way of fulfilling their own predictions, they could hardly be expected to give it enthusiastic support. Mr. Laing was made Convener of the first Committee appointed to work the new system, and he began operations under a double handicap. There was opposition to the new plan on its merits, and there was more or less friction in carrying out the details, as there always must be in putting any new plan into operation. Mr. Laing remained at the helm from 1865 to 1872, and then, perhaps, thinking that the work could be better done by some one who had not been connected with the new system in its unpopular days, he resigned, and Mr. Cochrane was appointed.* Mr. Cochrane had at that time been a member of the Committee for six

* Since the foregoing was in type the writer has learned that Dr. Laing resigned the convenership because he had ceased to be a pastor, having resigned his charge in Cobourg to do special work for Knox College.

years, and all that he knew about Home Mission work must have been learned on this Committee. He never did Home Mission work himself during his student days. In fact, at the time he was made Convener he was almost the only member of the Committee without experience in the Home Mission field. The members were: Wm. Cochrane, M.A. (Convener), John M. King, M.A., Wm. Burns, D. Paterson, A. J. Traver, John Burton, Wm. Donald, J. R. Scott, John Anderson, J. McColl, R. Torrance, R. H. Warden, Dr. Waters, F. McCuaig, Mungo Fraser, Dr. Proudfoot, C. C. Stewart, R. C. Moffatt, Prof. Bryce, Prof. Inglis, ministers; James Henderson, James Brown, T. McCrae, T. W. Taylor. Of this first Committee, over which Dr. Cochrane presided, many have gone to their reward. A very small number of them are on the Committee for 1899. Drs. Torrance and Warden, we believe, served with Dr. Cochrane from 1872 to the time of his death. Their long service, varied experience, and fine business ability were potent factors in making our Home Mission operations successful. Dr. Warden was Secretary of the Committee for many years, and when the Convenership became vacant through Dr. Cochrane's death, he was, as anybody would naturally expect, put into the Convener's chair.

The Home Mission work of the Presbyterian

Church in Canada has always had one great advantage over some of the other schemes. Most of the ministers who managed the Home work were Home missionaries in their student days. Of all the ministers who were members of the Home Mission Committee for the last twenty-five years, perhaps not one in fifty entered the ministry without doing some Home Mission work. Of all the ministers who managed our Foreign Mission work during the same period, perhaps not one in fifty ever saw a Foreign Mission station. The Home Committee, too, had the assistance of such experts as Dr. Robertson and Mr. Findlay, men who had spent the greater part of their lives on the Home field, and who knew every nook and corner of the territory under their care. Dr. Cochrane received, and deserved to receive, great credit for his services as Convener; but it is only fair to say that during his long and most successful labours he was aided by men of ability and experience, some of whom had expert knowledge of the mission fields under the care of the Committee.

The first year of Dr. Cochrane's convenership was not marked by any special features. The work was mainly confined to Ontario and Quebec, though operations had begun in Manitoba, where there was a College, and two missionaries supplied a number of stations around Winnipeg. Occasional supply was also given to Fort William during the summer months. It is substantially correct to say that when Dr. Cochrane became Convener, in 1872, the Home Mission field of the Church was bounded on the west by Lake Huron. When his labours ceased, in 1898, the western and north-western boundaries were the Pacific Ocean and the Yukon.

In 1872 the Students' Missionary Society of Knox College supplied four stations in the region around Sault Ste. Marie and Parry Sound. There are two Presbyteries in that region now. The Muskoka, Parry Sound and Nipissing Districts have congregations, or mission stations, at all points where a few Presbyterians can be gathered together. The best way, however, to get a correct idea of the work done is to look over a map of Northern Ontario and note the extent of the field from the Ottawa Valley to the Georgian Bay. That interesting stretch of new country is dotted with Presbyterian Home Mission stations. Then take a map of Manitoba, the North-West Territories and British Columbia, and as you run your eye westward over our splendid heritage, remember the Presbyterian Church has her missionaries in all parts of that immense region. Most of the stations and congregations were formed during the time that Dr. Cochrane was at the helm in Home Mission affairs.

It would be a great mistake, however, to suppose that the only Home Mission work done since 1872 was done in the new parts of the Dominion. New stations were organized and old ones helped in many parts of old Canada. Somebody once said that the American Presbyterian Church got on horseback and rode away west over the prairies and Rocky Mountains to the Pacific Coast and left many points behind at which useful work might have been done. Whether the Presbyterian Church in Canada ever got on horseback and rode west is a question that need not be discussed. One thing certain is that Presbyteries, aided by the Home Mission Committee, have been able to find a goodly number of points in old Canada at which promising mission stations could be opened with a fair prospect of growing into congregations. The suburban mission station, too, came into existence not so long ago. The Church made the discovery that a good, healthy, growing station can be organized on the outskirts of a city as well as in the new parts of the country.

In their Annual Report, submitted to the last General Assembly, the Home Mission Committee presented the following summary of the work done during Dr. Cochrane's convenership from 1875, the date of the last union, to the time of his death :

" As the data is not sufficiently definite for the years

prior to 1875, the comparison is made from that year —the year of the union of the Churches. There were then twenty-two Presbyteries in the Western Section of the Church, twenty-one of which were in the Provinces of Ontario and Quebec, and one west of Lake Superior. There were then under the care of the Committee 132 mission fields, including 267 preaching stations, with 127 missionaries, as also 86 supplemented congregations. The total revenue of the Fund in the year 1875-76, including not only Home Mission work but also the work of Augmentation, was $24,518.

"Now there are 41 Presbyteries in the Western Section of the Church—27 in the Provinces of Ontario and Quebec, and 14 west of Lake Superior. The number of mission fields at present reported is 384, with 1,116 preaching stations, and 468 missionaries, and the number of augmented congregations in the Western Section of the Church is 146. The revenue last year for both departments of the work amounted to $116,841, viz., $91,683 for Home Mission work proper, and $25,158 for Augmentation. The number of families connected with the missions and augmented congregations in 1875 was 7,243, now it exceeds 20,400.

"This statement, however, gives but a faint idea of the progress made in Home Mission work during these twenty-four years. Of the 132 mission fields that were connected with the Church in 1875, 59 have become self-supporting congregations, two have been merged into other fields, 34 have been raised to the status of augmented charges, 35 are still on the mission list, and two have ceased to exist.

"Since 1875, 590 new mission fields have been organized. Of this number 93 have been merged into others ; 297 are still on the mission list ; 58 have been raised to the status of augmented congregations ; and 142 have become self-supporting congregations, so that there are to-day 201 self-supporting congregations and 92 augmented charges, which in 1875 were either on the mission list or had no existence. In other words, during these twenty-four years the Home Mission Committee has fostered and helped to self-support 201 congregations, and raised to the status of augmented charges 92 mission fields—all of whom are in their turn giving liberal support, not only to the Home Mission work of the Church, but to every department of its work."

IN MANITOBA.

A year after his appointment to the convenership, Dr. Cochrane made his first visit to Manitoba. He and Dr. Ure were sent as commissioners to inquire into a movement that was being made by " certain parties in the town of Winnipeg" to open classes for higher education in Winnipeg. What this really meant was that the new college should be moved from Kildonan to Winnipeg. As the matter is now one of some historic interest, and as the result shows how wisely the Church has at times been led, we quote from the Minutes of Assembly for 1873:

"There was taken up and read a petition from certain parties in the town of Winnipeg, Manitoba, praying that the Senate of Manitoba College be empowered to make provision for the opening of classes for higher education in Winnipeg, in connection with the college, pledging themselves to find suitable accommodation in the meantime, and hoping that, in due season, buildings may be erected worthy of the Church, the College, and the advanced condition of the Province.

"There were read, also, a petition from inhabitants of the parish of Kildonan, Manitoba, representing the inexpediency and injustice of the proposals made in the former petition, and praying that the prayer of said petition be not granted, and that further measures be taken for the firmer establishment and fuller efficiency of the Manitoba College at Kildonan.

"Professor Bryce was heard in support of the petition for the opening of classes in connection with Manitoba College at Winnipeg.

"Mr. John Black was heard in support of the counter petition from the parish of Kildonan."

When Prof. Bryce and Mr. Black had finished their speeches, it was moved by Mr. J. Ross and seconded by Mr. R. Ure, "That the petition from Winnipeg, as to establishing classes for higher education in that town, by the Senate of Manitoba College, be not entertained."

"It was moved in amendment by Dr. Thornton, seconded by Mr. S. C. Fraser, 'That the petition be referred to a committee on the subject, with power to send for persons and papers.'" The amendment was carried, and after due deliberation the Committee recommended "That no change be now made, but that a commission of two be sent to inquire into the case and report to next Assembly; and, further, recommend that Messrs. Robert Ure and William Cochrane be that commission."

The commission was wisely chosen. Mr. Ure had been a warm friend of Mr. John Black, and was a safe man of much experience. Mr. Cochrane was Convener of the Home Mission Committee, and, besides being gifted in the useful art of settling disputes, was officially connected with the rapidly increasing Home Mission interests of Manitoba. The commission started early in July and spent nearly two months in Manitoba. The result of their mission was the removal of Manitoba College from Kildonan to Winnipeg. For particulars in regard to the manner in which the result was arrived at the reader is referred to the interesting reminiscences by Professor Bryce in another part of this volume.

All things considered, the removal of the college classes from Kildonan was perhaps the most delicate piece of work in which Dr. Cochrane engaged during the long period of his convenership. Presbyterians, especially Highland Scotch Presbyterians, are instinctively opposed to changes. Changing even the site of a church from one street to another, or from one concession to another, has often been found a serious matter. Kildonan had been the headquarters of Presbyterianism in the North-West for more than half a century. John Black, the pastor of Kildonan, had been a Presbyterian bishop for many years. To move the college away to Winnipeg, a town that up to that time had never been noted for righteousness and peace, seemed like sacrilege to a typical Kildonan man. But Bryce and Ure and Cochrane were wise men, and they did the right thing with as little friction as possible.

Professor Bryce has never got the credit he deserves for the part he took in this delicate and difficult piece of Church business. John Black was his first and best friend in Manitoba. Kildonan was his home, and much of the local support of the college came from Kildonan men. Mr. Bryce was a new man and a young man. The General Assembly was a long way from being a unit in favor of removal. People naturally sympathized with the veteran John Black, who had braved the hardships of the new country and alone preached the Gospel for years on the banks of the Red River. In the face of these and other obstacles Professor Bryce strenuously, but wisely, supported the movement for removal, and succeeded in accomplishing his purpose with the minimum of friction. Is there a man in the Presbyterian Church to-day who does not see that the Professor was right? Winnipeg is now a city with a population of over forty thousand, and the college has grown with the city. Notwithstanding their difference of opinion on the removal of the college, John Black and Professor Bryce remained the best of friends. Mr. Black and the men of Kildonan felt sore, but they stood loyally by the college, and Professor Bryce wrote Mr. Black's biography. In 1873 there were sixteen stations in the mission field of Manitoba, including Knox Church, Winnipeg. Travelling in Manitoba in those days was not done by rail; but, no doubt, the Convener covered the ground. He was then in his prime, the bracing air of the " Prairie Province" acted as a tonic on a system that little needed tonics, and we can easily understand that his visit was pleasant to himself and stimulating to the pioneers of Presbyterianism in Manitoba. A few weeks after his return to Ontario he went to Oakville and secured the assistance of one who proved a faithful helper until the end came twenty-five years afterwards.

In July, 1881, we find Dr. Cochrane again in Manitoba. The intervening eight years had been a growing time for the "Prairie Province." Winnipeg had grown from a straggling town of two or three thousand inhabitants to a city variously estimated, according to one of Dr. Cochrane's letters, " to contain from 10,000 to 13,000 inhabitants." The population of the province was growing. Presbyterianism was growing. The " boom " was growing, too, perhaps faster than anything else.

According to the statistics in the Presbyterian Blue Book, the Presbytery of Manitoba in 1873 had eight ministers. In 1881 it had twenty-nine ministers. The sixteen mission stations of 1873 had increased in number until the field extended well on toward the Rocky Mountains. Of course, the Convener of the Home Mission Committee was glad to see the work under his care progressing so well, and he showed his gratitude by hard work while on the ground. His visit lasted about three weeks, and here is the record : " Preached nine times, lectured three times, gave several addresses, attended meetings of Presbytery, visited out stations, and held consultations with the brethren."

One of the meetings of Presbytery is thus described in a letter written in Portage la Prairie at the time : " I left Winnipeg, Wednesday morning last, to attend a meeting of the Manitoba Presbytery at this point, some seventy miles west. On board our train we had no less than twelve members of Presbytery, principally from fields east of Winnipeg ; and at the Portage we met the western members, making in all an attendance of over twenty ministers, with several elders. In 1873, on my last visit, there were only some five or six ministers in the Presbytery, and hardly a congregation beyond Portage la Prairie. The Presbytery continued in session nearly three days, and but for the absolute necessity of adjournment on Friday, to enable as many as possible to reach their fields before Sabbath, the amount of important business before it might well have occupied a week. Some of the members came a distance of 150 miles to attend Presbytery, over roads, even at this season of the year, well nigh impassable. Many of these have the supervision of fields 100 miles in extent. No one in Ontario can have any idea of the greatness of our mission work in the North-West and its peculiar character, until he is face to face with the men who are labouring in such fields."

Two events of great interest to Presbyterians took place during this visit. Lord Lorne laid the foundation stone of Manitoba College, and the Rev. James Robertson, who had for seven years been pastor of Knox Church, Winnipeg, entered upon his great life-work as Superintendent of Home Missions for the North-West. Dr. Cochrane always claimed that he had "discovered Robertson." The discovery was a good one, whoever made it. Few ministers of any Church have been honoured to do work such as Dr. Robertson has done in laying the foundation of the Presbyterian Church in Manitoba and the North-West. By a strange coincidence the three men—Robertson, Cochrane and Bryce—whose names are inseparably connected with the growth of Presbyterianism in the "great lone land," were all from the Presbytery of Paris. Prof. Bryce never was a member of the Presbytery, but he was born and brought up within the bounds ; and his father, a worthy elder of Mount Pleasant when a member of the Presbytery, is perhaps the oldest member of the Court. Dr. Robertson was a hard working, successful pastor in Norwich before he went to Manitoba. The Paris Presbytery has no reason to be ashamed of its contribution to the work in the North-West.

Little need be said about Dr. Cochrane's remaining visits to Manitoba and the North-West. In his first two visits he helped to lay the foundation ; in subsequent tours he put stones on the wall.

In 1887, at the close of the meeting of Assembly in Winnipeg, he visited Birtle, Elkhorn, Banff, Regina, Portage la Prairie, and a number of other places, ending his tour at Port Arthur, where he spent Sabbath, July 17th.

Two years afterwards he visited Winnipeg, preached a number of times, but made no extended tour. His last visit to the capital of the "Prairie Province" was in June, 1897, when he attended the meeting of the General Assembly in that city. He came home as soon as the meeting of Assembly was over.

There was no city in the Dominion, except his own, that Dr. Cochrane liked better than he liked Winnipeg. He liked Winnipeg, and Winnipeg liked him. He had been closely identified with Presbyterian interests there from the first. Bryce and Robertson had been his neighbours in Ontario. He had many friends and old parishioners in the city. There were many reasons why he enjoyed visiting the Queen City of the West. In a closing paragraph in the "Life of John Black, the Apostle of the North," the author says :

" Not only in Winnipeg, with its thoroughly organized body of communicants, and in Portage la Prairie, Brandon, Regina and Calgary, have the Presbyterian views of Church doctrine and life become potential ; but in more than a score of towns, such as Morden, Pilot Mound, Deloraine, Carman, Glenboro', Treherne, Holland, Miami, Minnedosa, Russell, Rapid City, Gladstone, Moosomin, Prince Albert, Edmonton, Souris, Virden, Boissevain, Emerson, Keewatin, Rat Portage, Fort William and Port Arthur have strong, self-sustaining churches been established. Notably is the Church strongly ensconced in the affections of the agricultural communities spread over the prairies. It would gladden the heart of John Black to-day could he see the Presbytery of which he was the first Moderator now developed into two Synods with fourteen Presbyteries, and could he realize how 'the little one has become a thousand.' "

Dr. Cochrane lived to see the Presbytery of Manitoba—the one to which Dr. Bryce no doubt refers—grow into fourteen Presbyteries and two Synods. He not only saw the wonderful growth—he was a potent factor in causing it. A fifteenth Presbytery—the Presbytery of Kootenay—has been added since Dr. Cochrane's death. Few Presbyterians realize the magnitude of the work their Church has been honoured to do between Winnipeg and the Pacific Coast during the last twenty-five years.

IN MUSKOKA.

In the summer of 1878, Dr. Cochrane spent three weeks visiting the large mission field in the Presbytery of Barrie, known as Muskoka. Parry Sound was the first place visited, and perhaps it is as well to allow him to give the particulars himself, as he did in a letter to the *Canada Presbyterian*: " I preached in Parry Sound on Wednesday evening to a large congregation. In fact, we had two congregations, one that filled the church and another sitting on the rocks outside. The night was oppressively warm, and I am not sure but the rocky hearers had the best of it for once. The singing was hearty and the services impressive. We left on the following morning, to be succeeded on Sabbath by Dr. Robb, of Toronto, who preaches the anniversary sermons. As the great Methodist camp-meeting follows next week, we cannot imagine a better preparation for it than an eloquent and earnest exposition of Calvinistic Presbyterianism by our good brother of Cooke's Church, Toronto."

The imagination that led Dr. Cochrane to think of Dr. Robb's sermons as good preparation for a camp-meeting must have been made lively by the bracing air of the Georgian Bay.

From Parry Sound the Convener went to Rosseau;

from Rosseau to Bracebridge ; from Bracebridge to Huntsville—where he opened a new church, assisted by Mr. Findlay—and from Huntsville to Barrie, to attend a meeting of the Barrie Presbytery. The journey from Huntsville to the Presbytery is thus described : " A ride of six hours over a very rough road, with dangerous bridges, brought us to Bracebridge at 5 a.m. ; thence by boat to Gravenhurst at 7 a.m., and Barrie, by train, at eleven." After spending a day at the meeting of the Presbytery, he started for Sault Ste. Marie, Bruce Mines, and other places in that region.

During this tour Dr. Cochrane had good opportunities for forming an estimate of the work done by Mr. Findlay, Superintendent of Missions for Northern Ontario. He says: "Mr. Findlay has been of great service to us, as a Church, not only in his own pastorate but in taking a general superintendence of the mission field in the widely extended Muskoka District." Mr. Findlay, at that time, was pastor of the Bracebridge congregation, and gave four months of each year to the work of superintending the whole Muskoka field. A few years afterwards he was released from the pastorate, and his whole time has since been given to superintending the great mission field of Northern Ontario. Never did any servant of the Church work more faithfully in the face of many difficulties, and few have ever been honoured with greater success. Two new Presbyteries now work part of the field over which he tramped many a weary mile gathering the few early settlers together and forming them into mission stations. In concluding the letter from which we have quoted, Dr. Cochrane expresses the hope that Mr. Findlay "may be long spared to the Church in this important and laborious field." Every man who knows the value of Mr. Findlay's services, and who knows the importance of New Ontario as a mission field, will "associate" himself, as Sir Wilfrid Laurier would say, with this hope. Mr. Findlay has suffered from one cruel disability throughout the whole of his ministry—he has absolutely no capacity for blowing his own trumpet.

About this time there were distinct intimations that Dr. Cochrane was beginning to feel the effects of overwork. On the last day of August, immediately after his return from Muskoka, he wrote: "Since my return from my tour have been used up more than ever before. Have no heart for work of any kind, and the amount lying before me to do is dreadful. I can neither write nor study. College, above all, worries me."

In August, 1881, Dr. Cochrane made a short visit to Muskoka and "opened a new church and lectured," and had some further experience of Muskoka roads in the early days. "Had a severe shaking from Bracebridge to Port Sydney and back again, and lost a good many things out of my valise, which broke open on the way."

Four years later he visited Midland and Parry Sound, and preached and lectured at the latter place.

These visits to the Muskoka field touched most of the leading points of that time. Since then many new stations have been opened. Some have grown into augmented congregations, and some augmented congregations have become self-sustaining congregations. Two new Presbyteries have been formed north of the Presbyteries of Barrie and Owen Sound, and when New Ontario is more fully peopled the Church must follow the settler and the miner.

IN BRITISH COLUMBIA.

In the summer of 1882, after his election to the Moderatorship of the General Assembly, Dr. Cochrane visited British Columbia, partly on Home Mission business and partly to see what could be done in the way of inducing the Presbyterians of British Columbia, connected with the Church of Scotland, to join the Presbyterian Church in Canada. The Session of Zion Church gave him a good "send-off," and the Presbyterians of British Columbia a hearty welcome. He visited Victoria, New Westminster, Yale,

Nanaimo, Langley, and other places, and did all in his power to encourage the people by sermons and addresses. No good purpose would be served by giving details of the negotiations which led to the union of all the Presbyterian interests on the coast. There is only one Presbyterian Church there now; and, as Dr. Bryce says in his reminiscences, Dr. Cochrane's visit was largely instrumental in bringing about this happy result. In no place that he ever visited did he receive a heartier welcome than in British Columbia.

In June, 1887, after attending the meeting of the General Assembly in Winnipeg, he went a second time to the coast and visited Vancouver, Victoria, Nanaimo, Wellington Mines, and other places. In November, 1890, he made a third visit, preached eight times, lectured six times, delivered nine addresses, and brought home three British Columbia girls for the Young Ladies' College.

The foregoing are specimens of Dr. Cochrane's work on the three great mission fields of the Presbyterian Church—Muskoka, Manitoba and the North-West Territories, and British Columbia. No doubt other places were visited, but the services rendered on the great fields are quite sufficient to illustrate the Convener's activity and working power.

It is almost impossible to over-estimate the value of a visit by a strong minister—a man of faith and power—to a young, struggling mission station or congregation. Dr. Wardrope's visits in the Ottawa valley in the early days are remembered to this day. Dr. Burns lifted many a struggling cause on his tours through north-western Ontario, and gave fresh life and hope to the people. No doubt Dr. Cochrane's many missionary tours had the same effect.

Having looked at part of Dr. Cochrane's work on the Home Mission field, it may now be useful to glance at some of his work done for Home Missions in the older congregations of the Church.

ADDRESSES.

There is no way of ascertaining the exact value of a missionary address, nor, for that matter, the exact value of any given sermon. Speaking generally, the addresses on Home Missions delivered by Dr. Cochrane in many places for many years must have done much to increase the interest of the people in Home Mission work and to stimulate their liberality. He spoke on many platforms, chiefly between Montreal and Lake Huron, and his speeches were always instructive and often rousing. The people liked to hear Cochrane, as his friends familiarly called him, and however weak and wearied he may have been, his speeches on Home Missions rarely, if ever, disappointed them. He had the subject at his finger ends, and could lay the work and its claims before an audience in popular style.   There was a certain audacity about Dr. Cochrane's oratory that added much to his effectiveness, and enabled him to say things that no other man could say with impunity.   If any other speaker had told an audience composed largely of Scotch Presbyterians that half farthings were first coined to give certain kinds of Scotchmen an opportunity to contribute to charitable and religious purposes, there might have been trouble ; but when Cochrane said so they always laughed, and sometimes applauded.   His frequent tours in Manitoba, the North-West Territories and British Columbia, gave him an immense advantage in speaking on Home Missions.   The man who has been on the ground and has got his information at first hand always has advantages over the man who has merely read or heard.   Many Presbyterians had friends or relatives in the prairie country, or on the coast, and naturally they wished to hear about that part of the Dominion.   Many more wished to go west themselves, and, of course, they were anxious to learn as much as possible about what might become their future home.   All things considered, the Convener of the Home Mission Committee had great opportunities on the missionary platform, and he made the most of them in the interests of the Church.

Though at the head of the Home Mission work, Dr.

Cochrane was the reverse of a narrow, bitter specialist. He never disparaged or belittled the other schemes of his Church. Usually be began his speeches by commending, as a loyal Presbyterian, all the other schemes to his audience, and then he went fully into the special work that the Church had assigned to him as Convener of one of her most important committees.

LETTERS.

Perhaps the platform part of his Home Mission work was the part the Convener liked most. The letter writing was, undoubtedly, the part he disliked most, and no wonder if he did dislike it. No matter how sick or weary he may have been when he came home—and he nearly always came home from a tour suffering from a cold—there was the inevitable pile of letters to answer. That the subject matter of some of them was not worth the paper they were written on —to say nothing of the postage stamp—may be taken for granted. Still they had to be answered. Long letters, not connected in any way with his duties as Convener, had to be replied to, or the Convener would certainly be accused of neglect, perhaps of discourtesy. "Wrote twenty letters, chiefly on Home Missions"; "wrote thirty letters, chiefly on Home Mission business"; "wrote a multitude of letters chiefly on Home Mission business." These are the entries that you find every week in his diary. Whatever else is omitted, the pile of letters is always there. And the worst feature of the case was that the pile had usually accumulated during the early part of the week, when Dr. Cochrane was from home, and had to be attacked on Friday or Saturday, when he wished to be at work on his sermons. To stand that kind of work for a few weeks is hard enough, but to stand it for all the weeks of a quarter of a century is killing.

REPORTS.

If all the reports on Home Mission work prepared by Dr. Cochrane and presented by him to the General Assembly were bound, the volume would contain all the information needed in regard to the early history of Presbyterianism in the newer parts of the Dominion. The book would not be a popular one, but it might be useful. Dr. Torrance would enjoy it immensely, and use it with great benefit to the Church in making comparisons and striking averages.

For clearness, for good arrangement of facts and of figures, for information given in a condensed form, for presentation of the whole work without wearisome details, Dr. Cochrane's annual reports were models. No annual statements prepared in Canada, not even the statements made by the highest bank managers, displayed more business ability than was displayed

9

in the annual reports of our Home Mission Committee. We never were behind the scenes in the Home Mission, nor any other Committee of the Church, and assume that the work on the Annual Report was done mainly, if not exclusively, by Dr. Cochrane himself. We know he usually began about the end of March and worked on the report until he got it ready for the General Assembly. Many a Home Mission orator got his ammunition from these reports.

During the last ten years of his life Dr. Cochrane was assisted in his Home Mission and other correspondence by his only daughter. Mary, as her father always called her, was an expert type-writer and clever general secretary. She inherited much of her father's capacity for business, and was most helpful to him in his voluminous correspondence. Miss Cochrane knows more about the inner history of the Presbyterianism of Western Canada than is known by most ministers of the Church.

Mention should be made of Dr. Cochrane's services in securing liberal grants for Home Mission work from Presbyterian churches in Great Britain. The Colonial Committee of the Free Church of Scotland passed the following resolution a few weeks after his death :

"The Committee have learned with profound regret of the death of the Rev. Dr. Cochrane, Convener of the Home Mission Committee of the Presbyterian Church in Canada, and they desire to place on record their sense of his distinguished services in connection with the spread of the Gospel throughout the Dominion. The remarkable energy and enthusiasm, the stirring eloquence and administrative capacity, which he brought to this most important enterprise, rendered Dr. Cochrane's name a household word in Canada, and won for him the esteem and gratitude of the Church at home. This Committee have to acknowledge their indebtedness to him during the past twenty-five years for his admirable reports of Home Mission work, for his wise counsel, and for the inspiration of his untiring zeal. They would heartily assure the brethren in Canada of their sympathy with them in the great loss which the Church there has sustained through the removal of this eminent minister, and their earnest prayer that it may please God to sanctify the event to the furtherance of the Gospel in all parts of the Dominion."

The Colonial Committee of the Free Church of Scotland does not pass resolutions like this one without good reason for so doing. The youth of twenty-three who left Paisley in 1854 had made his influence felt on one of the great Churches of his native land.

CHAPTER VI.

Various kinds of work—On the press—In the Church Courts
—On commissions—Volumes published—The Pan-Presbyterian Alliance—The Young Ladies' College.

HAD Dr. Cochrane not been a minister of the
Gospel, in all probability he would have been
the editor of a daily newspaper, or the head of a
publishing house. He liked books and reviews and
magazines, and he read with avidity all kinds of
newspapers. "Rose at seven and got the papers," is
an entry often found in his diary. He had, in large
measure, the journalistic instinct. Letters written
when he was a mere lad in Paisley show that he had
acquired a clear, crisp, pungent style. He read standard literature generously, but he never forgot the
daily papers. Essays were read in the societies with
which he was connected in Paisley, and, of course,
young Cochrane did his full share in the way of
production and criticism. Reports of the meetings
were frequently written by him, and nothing is more
probable than that he furnished an occasional paragraph for a friendly journal. A bright, ambitious

young man who reads newspapers as Dr. Cochrane did in early life is very likely to try his hand at writing for them if the editors give him any encouragement, which the editors always do if the youth can make the right kind of "copy." During his college days Dr. Cochrane was a voluminous writer of letters. In Hanover he wrote some poetry which he always described in his diary as "doggerel." If he did not at that time, and during his pastorate in Jersey City, write something for the press, he was in that particular unlike most young men of his type and very unlike himself.

Thirty years ago the Stratford *Beacon* was said to be the best weekly paper in the Dominion. Mr. William Buckingham, its proprietor and editor, was an accomplished and resourceful journalist, a man of culture and a good man of business—qualities not always found together. Like a true journalist, he was always on the look out for writers who could give distinctive features to his journal. The late Dr. Waters, then a pastor in St. Mary's, was asked to contribute a serial story, and Dr. Cochrane, who was making his influence felt around Brantford, was engaged to furnish signed contributions. The story never appeared, but the contributions came for three or four years and sent the circulation of the *Beacon* up among the Presbyterians, the result, no doubt, at which the enterprising editor was aiming. How much Dr. Cochrane wrote for the Brantford papers and papers published elsewhere may never be known. There is some reason to believe that he used the editorial "we" occasionally in quarters highly influential.

Wherever Dr. Cochrane went to assist in doing any kind of public work for the Church, he usually wrote a report of the proceedings for the press, if no regular reporters were present. He did so on principle. He held that the public should know what the Church is doing. He believed that the world is the better for knowing all about Church operations, and that it is the duty of the Church to make her work known. Who will contend that Dr. Cochrane's theory was not the right one? Is there one official in the Church responsible for the working of any scheme who does not try, in every proper way, to lay his scheme before the public? Would our Church work go on better if we concealed it from the public? There is a good opportunity to make an experiment of that kind at the present time. Try the occult plan with the Century Fund and see how long it will take for the million to come in. Dr. Cochrane held that a Church, governed by the people and supported by the people, should tell the people what it is doing and what it wants them to do, and he practised his own theory, which is more than some theorists do. If he took part in the induction of a minister, or the opening of a Church, or any other work of that kind, he often wrote a report of the services for the local and Church papers. As Clerk of his Synod and Presbytery, he always made a synopsis of the proceedings for the press. He was an expert at that kind of work. He wrote with marvellous rapidity ; his "copy" was clean, neat, and legible, and was ready for the printer as soon as the meeting was over.

During his vacations, and when on missionary tours, he usually wrote descriptive letters for the press. In 1888 he sent seven letters to the *Globe*, giving an account of the meeting of the Pan-Presbyterian Council in London; and in 1884 five, describing the meeting of that body in Belfast. His letters from Manitoba and the North-West were much enjoyed by readers in old Canada. Twenty-five years ago Winnipeg seemed as far away as the Yukon appears to be now. People in Eastern Canada were very anxious to know something of the "great lone land," which has since provided a home for many of them. Trustworthy information was not easily obtained. Dr. Bryce and Mr. MacBeth were not then writing books. By his lectures and descriptive letters Dr. Cochrane did good service in giving the people of old Canada trustworthy information about our great possessions in the North-West.

Perhaps Dr. Cochrane's best literary work was done on his earlier lectures. He wrote in all about twenty, each one long enough to take two hours or more in delivery. Those written when he was not over-burdened with other work, when his style was not impaired by too much writing and speaking, are genuine works of art. The arrangement of matter is often skilful, and the literary execution high class. In fact, some of them are rather too well composed for popular delivery. The penmanship is like copper-plate, each page a thing of beauty. Comparing his handwriting in these earlier lectures with the penman-ship of his diary for the last year or two, one sees with painful vividness the difference between a man in the full vigour of bounding life and a man weary and worn with excessive toil.

During his pastorate in Brantford Dr. Cochrane published five volumes: "The Heavenly Vision," "Christ and Christian Life," "The Church and the Commonwealth," "Future Punishment," and "Me-moirs and Remains" of his friend, the Rev. Walter Inglis, of Ayr. The first three volumes are sermons selected from his ordinary preparations for the pulpit of Zion Church. There is no reason to suppose that they are much, if anything, better than many other sermons that he preached in the usual course of his ministry. Quite likely he himself thought they were among his best; but preachers are not infallible judges of their own pulpit work. Perhaps some of the good people in Zion Church could tell of sermons that they considered much more effective than any their pastor published.

Taking these three volumes of sermons as a whole, they have two distinguishing characteristics : One is their high average of excellence, and the other their pronounced evangelical tone. Soon after the publication of one of these volumes a prominent minister and Professor of Theology, who has since gone to his rest, said there was " almost no minister in the Presbyterian Church who made as high an average in the pulpit" as was made by Dr. Cochrane. The average is the real test. Some of the most worthless men that enter the pulpit can preach even brilliant sermons when they are after a call.

Besides his published volumes, many other sermons preached by Dr. Cochrane found their way into print. His memorial sermons and annual sermons to the Scotchmen of Brantford would make a bulky volume.

There is no reason to doubt that Dr. Cochrane could have made a substantial, perhaps permanent, contribution to literature, had he not been burdened with an amount and kind of work that made success in literary work an impossibility. Copying and engrossing the minutes of Church Courts does not improve one's literary taste. Writing innumerable letters, many of them about the most trivial matters, is not an intellectual tonic.   There is a large amount of work in a Home Mission report, but it is not a kind of literature that the reading public care much for.   In fact, it was Dr. Cochrane's duty to spend much time and strength in writing what he must have known hardly anybody wants to read.   Writing for the dusty shelf of a book case, or for the waste paper basket, is not a stimulating kind of literary work.

IN THE CHURCH COURTS.

It is difficult for one who sat in the same Presbytery with Dr. Cochrane for eleven years, and in the same Synod for seven, to deal with him fairly as a member of the Church Courts without the appearance of fulsome eulogy. Self-respect and respect for his memory alike forbid anything of the kind, to say nothing of the respect due to one's readers. Justice, even cold justice, willingly assigns Dr. Cochrane a first place as an ecclesiastical administrator and jurist.

To begin with, he attended the Church Courts with marked regularity, and that is a good deal in this age and country. The work in an average Church Court usually falls upon a few, and Dr. Cochrane was always one of the few. There was no kind of administrative or judicial work that he could not do, and he was always willing to do it. Natural aptitude and a long business training in Paisley, combined with much experience in the Church Courts, gave him many advantages not possessed by the average Presbyter. He thoroughly believed in the Presbyterian form of Church government. He saw no necessary antagonism between constituted authority and wholesome personal liberty. The liberty of the private member of the Church was, in his opinion, not assailed nor minimized, but safeguarded by good laws wisely administered. Believing this, he went about his duties in the Presbytery with as much earnestness and with as great a sense of responsibility as he entered the pulpit. His fourteen years of service as clerk of the Presbytery of Paris, and over twenty as clerk of the Synod of Hamilton and London, were of great use to the Church. His Presbytery often sent him to prosecute calls, a line of work in which he became an expert, though he sometimes found his duties the reverse of pleasant.

Dr. Cochrane had a seat in almost every General Assembly. He was often appointed Secretary or Convener of the Committee on Bills and Overtures, the committee that arranges the work for the Supreme Court. This, with the Home Mission Report, and the Report of the Young Ladies' College, and the active part he always took in other business, made attendance at the Assembly for him anything but a holiday.

It was much easier for Dr. Cochrane to be an active and useful member of the Church Courts than it is for some other Presbyters. He had a natural aptitude for business. He was a natural-born Churchman, and his Church was the Presbyterian. From his earliest days he had been accustomed to take an active part in Church affairs. Like most Scotchmen, and all Paisley men, he enjoyed ecclesiastical discussion. Seldom did he look happier than when he took his favourite position in the corner of a pew at a meeting of Presbytery or Assembly, rested his head against the top of the pew, fumbled his long gold chain, and listened with a smile as the brethren threshed out some difficult question.

ON COMMISSIONS.

Dr. Cochrane had not a judicial manner. Dr. McLaren or Dr. Warden might pass for a judge on the street, but nobody would pick Dr. Cochrane out of a crowd and say he was a chief justice. His gait was too rapid, his utterance too quick, and his whole manner too breezy to suggest the Bench. And yet, in the unpleasant work of inquiring into and settling those wretched quarrels that too often arise in congregations, he perhaps never had a superior in the Church. Knowing this, his Synod and Presbytery seldom, if ever, failed to put him on commissions for judicial purposes. He had seen enough of the world to know that every story has two sides. He was not in the least degree afflicted with the infirmity which leads so many ministers to believe everything told them in pious tones. Better than most men did he know how to discount a statement made in anger, or an inference drawn in malice. In the art of putting questions, a truthful answer to which would throw a flash of light on the point at issue, he was an expert. His strongest point, however, in judicial work was his skill in drawing up a deliverance at the close of an inquiry, that seemed to settle the case and satisfy all reasonable parties. Other men could discourse on the difficulty, but Cochrane could show the way out —if anybody could. To mention cases in which he displayed rare skill as a peacemaker might stir up the ashes of old difficulties. Suffice it to say that Dr. Cochrane was an invaluable member of a judicial commission.

An extract from his diary will show some of the difficulties ministers had to contend against when doing judicial work about thirty years ago:

"Started for Goderich at 10 a.m. At Stratford took dinner with Buckingham, of the *Beacon*, and started again at 2. All the members of the commission with us. Left Goderich for Lucknow at 6 p.m., in a covered stage on runners, in a blinding snow-storm. We were crowded—eight of us—into space usually allotted to six. It was black as midnight, and had it not been for careful driving and a kind Providence we would certainly have met with an accident. The wind blew a perfect hurricane from Lake Huron, and indicated an awful night, as it turned out before we reached Lucknow. When half-way we stuck in a snow-drift, and had all to get out except ——, who kept comfortably within. On a few miles, and again we all got out and lifted the stage out of the snowbank. In the midst of all we kept ourselves as cheerful as possible. Discussed theology and Church government, and shared some bread and cheese that Mr. McQuarrie had brought with him from Goderich. Finally, about 11 p.m., we reached Lucknow, wearied and hungry. Had supper, and then, after worship, to bed."

Mention has been made of Dr. Cochrane's great resources in settling difficulties. It is needless to say that in doing so he was conspicuously fair. His was a keen sense of justice, and he not only saw the right, but he did it.

PAN-PRESBYTERIAN ALLIANCE.

Dr. Cochrane was chosen to represent his Church at three meetings of the Pan-Presbyterian Alliance—

in Belfast in 1884, in London in 1888, and in Glasgow in 1896. He was chairman for many years of the Sabbath School Committee of the Alliance, and read the Sabbath School Report at the meeting in Glasgow—the last one he attended. He was for many years a member of the Executive Commission of the Western or American Section, and on the death of his friend, Dr. Waters, in 1897, was appointed Recording Secretary. He had arranged to go with Dr. Warden to a meeting of the Executive Commission in St. Louis the week in which he was laid to rest. To a man of books, such as Dr. Cochrane was, a meeting of the Alliance must have been a rare source of enjoyment, not so much on account of the business as for another reason. A lover of books always likes to see men who have written books. A meeting of the Alliance is one of the best places in the world to see authors of the highest class.

The day after his death the following letter was written by the Secretary to Sheriff Watt:

Mr. William Watt, jun.,
        Brantford, Ont., Canada:

Dear Sir,—Your telegram announcing the sudden death of Dr. Cochrane came to hand this morning. This unexpected event gives a great shock to one's deepest sensibilities. Kindly tender my sincerest sympathies to the bereaved family, and also my sharp sense of the overshadowing bereavement suffered by the congregation at Brantford, and by the Presbyterian Church of Canada. Dr. Cochrane had attached himself by strong ties of friendship to the Churches in the United States. They recognized in him a leader in the cause of our common Saviour, and valued him highly for his most excellent qualities, both of mind and heart. He was further deeply interested in the work of the Alliance, and by his earnest and consecrated life greatly aided in bringing the Presbyterian and Reformed Churches, both on this continent and throughout the world, into larger realization of their true unity and of their common work. May the Lord comfort all who are bereaved by his death, and may God grant that the mantle of this Elijah may soon rest upon the shoulders of an Elisha.

With sincere esteem,
Yours very truly,
Wm. Henry Roberts,
Secretary.

Mrs. Cochrane was also kindly remembered by friends in the United States, as well as by hundreds at home. Letters like the following should remind us that Christians are one the world over:

Philadelphia, Pa., Nov. 4th, 1898.

Mrs. Wm. Cochrane,

Brantford, Ont., Canada:

Dear Madam,—Your beloved and sainted husband was associated with the work of the Presby terian Alliance from its first beginnings. He rendered admirable service, was highly appreciated by his brethren, and by none more so than by myself. At the last meeting of the Executive Commission, which your husband had arranged to attend, and from which he was greatly missed, the minutes herewith enclosed was adopted by the members present. I transmit the same to you, accompanied with the expression of warm personal sympathy for yourself, and of the highest regard for your husband and my friend.

With sincere esteem,
Very truly yours,
Wm. Henry Roberts.

The resolution referred to in the foregoing letter shows the position which Dr. Cochrane held as a member of the Alliance :—

Extract from the minutes of the Western Section of the Executive Commission of the Alliance of the Reformed Churches throughout the world holding the Presbyterian System, at its meeting October 27th, 1898, at St. Louis, Mo. :

"The Commission records its deep sense of the loss sustained in the removal by death of the late Rev. William Cochrane, D.D., of Brantford, Ont., Canada, whose devotion to the work of the Alliance it gratefully recognizes.

"Dr. Cochrane was a member of, and took an active part in, every meeting of the General Council,

As chairman for many years of the Sabbath School Committee of the Alliance, and more recently as the Recording Secretary of the Western Section of the Executive Commission, Dr. Cochrane rendered special service. By his genial disposition and kindly presence he endeared himself personally to the brethren, by whom his memory is fondly cherished."

Attest,

Wm. Henry Roberts,

Secretary.

THE YOUNG LADIES' COLLEGE.

In 1874 Dr. Cochrane and several other public-spirited citizens of Brantford came to the conclusion, no doubt after due investigation, that there was an opening for a young ladies' college in this part of the Dominion. Naturally enough, they also concluded that Brantford was the best location for the institution. Though non-sectarian, the college was to be connected with the Presbyterian Church. An annual report, usually presented by Dr. Cochrane, has always been made to the General Assembly, and the Assembly has, at least nominally, appointed the directors.

The management of a ladies' college was a much more difficult matter in Ontario a quarter of a century ago than it has since become. High-class teachers were not so easily secured as they are now. The number of people who knew much by experience about the internal working of institutions of that kind was limited. There was also an easily ascertained limit to the number of people who could afford to send their daughters to an institution like the Young Ladies' College of Brantford. Perhaps this was the most serious limit of all.

Dr. Cochrane was one of the founders of the institution; he was President of the Board of Management for many years; he taught classes every session, and was Governor of the College when he died. Through his influence many students were brought to the institution, and he displayed a paternal interest in all those that studied within its walls. It is quite safe to say there were many times when the College gave Dr. Cochrane more anxiety, if not more actual work, than either Zion Church or the Convenership of the Home Mission Committee gave him. When a student in Princeton, he came to the conclusion that "Scotch congregations in America are ticklish stuff." Later on, perhaps, he concluded that Scotch congregations are not the only institutions somewhat difficult to manage.

CHAPTER VII

Dr. Cochrane as a citizen—His first vote in America—
Interest in public affairs—His political creed.

"VOTED as usual," is the entry often found in
Dr. Cochrane's diary on the first Monday of
January. Sometimes the names of the persons are
given that he voted for, and in one instance he says :
"Voted for Mayor, Aldermen, School Trustees, money
by-law—everything." So far as voting was concerned
he described his practice well when he said, "voted
for everything." He had a feeling of utter contempt
for the theory that a minister of the Gospel should
not take any part in public affairs. That theory
might do for Plymouth, but it never took root in
Paisley. From his earliest days he had been accustomed to take an interest in all public matters, and it
never dawned on his mind for a moment that because
he was a minister he should lessen his interest in the
affairs of the country, and of his own community in
particular. He voted on the first Monday in January
for "everything," and never made any explanation for
so doing. He voted at every political election as a

plain matter of duty, and never apologized for exercising his rights as a citizen and doing his duty.

Dr. Cochrane's first duties as a citizen in America were not much to his liking. There was a municipal regulation at Hanover which made it compulsory for all citizens to do what we in Ontario call "statute labour." In May, 1856, the student from Paisley had to discharge this elementary duty of citizenship, and this is what he said about it at the time: "Worked at the roads all day from 8 till 4, and have to do so again to-morrow. This is one of the blessings of a free country and a free government—one of the privileges of Democracy and Republicanism. It is a scandalous shame and gross imposition to compel students to make roads and ditches; however, as I wish to be a good citizen of whatever country I inhabit, I never object to obey, for the general good. The day was very warm and oppressive, but we got along very well. When I started out in the morning I was fully determined to do as little as possible, but once at it I worked hard. I don't like to do anything by halves. The classes called out were the Senior and Junior, and we had some good jokes between us."

The spectacle of Dr. Cochrane doing "roadwork" is amusing, but it is highly suggestive. We see a young citizen willing to endure for the "general good," and we get a flash of light which reveals the secret of his success in life; he never did "anything by halves," not even "roadwork."

In October of the same year he became a citizen of the United States, and soon afterwards gave his first vote. It grieved him much to give up his citizenship as a British subject, but the reason why he did so was highly creditable. "I once thought that I never would naturalize; but the times so imperiously demand a united front against slavery that I felt bound in conscience to add my vote to the cause of freedom." A few days afterwards the vote was "added" at the election of State Officers, but it was not polled without some friction. "Studied till ten and then went and voted the Republican ticket. ——, an old liner, and one of our so-called 'Whiskey Democrats,' challenged my vote. I soon, however, made it legal by taking the oath and showing the necessary documents. I felt quite mad at the old *scamp*, who knew quite well that I would not attempt to vote *illegally*, and that his challenge was useless."

A few days afterwards he voted the Republican ticket at the Presidential election, but his vote was not challenged. Fifteen years afterwards, however, he had the doubtful pleasure of again defending his vote at the polls. In the Provincial election of March, 1871, the scrutineer acting for the Hon. E. B.

Wood, challenged his vote. His comment on this second experience is quite as vigorous as the one he made in Hanover. What he thought a few years afterwards, when his own party made Mr. Wood a Chief Justice, is not on record.

In everything that pertained to the welfare of Brantford Dr. Cochrane took a lively interest. He loved his own city and felt rather proud of being a Brantford man. He was not a citizen of Brantford because he could find no other place to live in. He was often asked to go elsewhere, but he preferred dwelling with his own people and doing all in his power to advance the higher interests of his own city. He took much interest in the schools of the city, in the Mechanics' Institute, in the Hospital, in the Institute for the Blind, and in all public institutions.

In politics Dr. Cochrane was a Liberal, though by no means a Paisley Radical. Were he in England to-day Rosebery would likely be his leader. In the United States his intense hatred of slavery made him a pronounced Republican. George Brown was the public man in Canada that he admired most; nor was the admiration by any means lost. When the Senator resided at Bow Park he was Dr. Cochrane's parishioner. George Brown admired energy in the pulpit as well as in every other sphere of activity, and his Brantford pastor gave him as energetic preaching as his heart could desire. Dr. Cochrane had also a most profound respect for Alexander Mackenzie. He had frequently been a guest in Mr. Mackenzie's house, and like all other good men who came in contact with Alexander Mackenzie in private, he felt the influence of his strong and wholesome personality. Of course, a man who cultivated, as Dr. Cochrane did, the noble art of settling difficulties, could not fail to admire Sir Oliver Mowat's marvellous skill in dealing with difficult problems. If there was one thing that Dr. Cochrane prided himself in it was his skill in smoothing out wrinkles in Church matters. He envied Sir Oliver's capacity for smoothing out wrinkles in the State. As a Brantford man, he was pleased to see Messrs. Paterson and Hardy promoted, and he would have been the first to offer congratulations if a neighbour of any party had received similar promotion.

Dr. Cochrane was a Liberal; but let no reader suppose that he was a blind partisan. He saw weak points in his own party, just as he saw weak points in his own Church, and he was always willing to give ample credit to other parties for any good thing they did or attempted to do. He never allowed politics to interfere in the slightest degree with his personal, social or ecclesiastical relations. Some of his oldest and warmest friends were not of the party with which he voted. As became a Paisley man, he believed in free discussion and British fair play. Any attempt to tamper with the rights of any citizen roused his indignation. Few men had a keener sense of justice. "Fight hard as you please, but fight fair," was his motto in all political and municipal contests.

Dr. Cochrane gave no explanation, made no apology, for discharging any duties as a citizen that he thought proper to discharge. He questioned no other elector's right to vote, and he took precious good care that no other elector interfered with him. He was a manly citizen, courageous to the finger-tips. Even his Church was not allowed to influence him in matters pertaining to the State. A friend once asked him what effect the resolutions passed by the Church Courts in regard to the Jesuits' Estates Act and kindred matters would have upon his vote. His characteristic reply was: "Tut! I'll vote for Paterson just the same."

A man's fellow-citizens are the best judges of his merits as a citizen. The days that Dr. Cochrane's body lay in state, and the afternoon on which it was carried to its last resting-place, the people of Brantford gave their verdict as to the character of his citizenship for thirty-six years. In the most unmistakable manner they said he had been a good citizen.

CHAPTER VIII.

At his last meeting of the Home Mission Committee—Illness—Sudden death—Funeral services—Addresses by several ministers.

ON Monday, the 10th day of October, 1898, one week before his death, Dr. Cochrane went to Toronto to preside over his last meeting of the Home Mission Committee. The meeting took place on the following day, and a considerable amount of business was done. Was Dr. Cochrane seriously ill when he presided over that meeting? Those who met with him saw no symptoms of serious illness, but that proves nothing either way. His power for concealing weakness or illness until he finished his day's work was marvellous. To one or two friends he complained of weariness, but he was often weary. His physical condition when he met the Home Mission Committee for the last time must be decided, not by what others saw or did not notice, not by what he may have said casually to some of his friends, but by his medical advisers, who certainly were the best judges. Dr. Nichol, who was long and intimately associated with him in Church and college work, writes : " It was my privilege to be long and intimately associated with him in Church and college work. I noticed no symptoms of breaking down till about a year before his death. I would not say he had a robust constitution, but he was wiry to the extreme, and would go through an amount of work that would prostrate any two men, and show but little fatigue till his task was done. His power of recuperation was truly marvellous. Repeatedly have I known him almost exhausted in the pulpit, but rallying again in a few days."

Dr. Philip, a well-known physician of Brantford, an ex-president of the Ontario Medical Council, and for many years his trusted medical attendant, writes: " In reference to the physical constitution of the late Dr. Cochrane, I would say that although his physique was slight and his muscular development much below the average, still he was wiry (if I may use the term), and was able to undergo for many years during the most active part of his ministry an immense amount of physical work and fatigue. He had no *organic* disease of any kind apparent until a few months before his death. I have no doubt that, had he conserved the physical powers with which he was endowed, to even a moderate extent, he might in all human probability have outlived the allotted span. But you know his restless nature, ever on the wing, ever at work, until, as was to be expected, he had exhausted his capital of strength, and the end came somewhat unexpectedly at the last."

The testimony of these medical gentlemen makes it quite clear that the final break-down in Dr. Cochrane's health began about a year before his death. He himself thought it began at a much earlier period, and many a time recorded the fact in his diary. Too much importance, however, must not be attached to what a sensitive man thinks about his health in a time of extreme weakness or weariness. Most men of a nervous, sensitive temperament in times of extreme depression think their end is near. It is idle to speak of what might have been had Dr. Cochrane unloaded himself of all extra work a few years ago, as Dr. Philip and other friends often urged him to do. For reasons which at least partially satisfied himself, he did not do so, and the end came with alarming suddenness.

On Wednesday, the 12th, he returned to Brantford and on his arrival learned that Mrs. Cochrane's sister, Mrs. Sheriff Watt, had died that forenoon. Mrs. Watt was a lovely character. Her quiet, gentle disposition, her kindly spirit, and the patience and courage with which she had for years endured severe illness that deprived her of the power of speech, endeared her to a large circle of friends. Wednesday afternoon was partly spent by Dr. Cochrane in helping to make arrangements for the funeral, and in the evening he addressed his prayer meeting as usual. Thursday was given to pastoral visitation. Friday he officiated at Mrs. Watt's funeral, assisted by his neighbour, Mr. Hamilton, of the First Presbyterian Church. Friday evening was spent at home, and he complained of being "very tired and worn out." Saturday he prepared the sermon on 1 Peter i. 6, which is published in this volume. On the outside of the first leaf he wrote the title and the date at which he expected the sermon to be delivered, in the following order :

IF NEED BE.

Brantford, Oct. 16, 1898.　　　　　　　　*1 Peter i. 6.*

This sermon was intended for Sabbath evening. Along with it, lying in his desk, was found another intended for Sabbath morning, the text being Psalm cxix. 54, and the title, "The Pilgrim's Song." The inscription was in the same order as that on the sermon intended for the evening :

THE PILGRIM'S SONG.

Brantford, Oct. 16, 1898.　　　　　　　　*Psalm cxix. 54.*

The evening sermon was probably begun and finished on Saturday, and the morning one, not quite

so fully written out, was probably prepared at different times during the week as other duties permitted.
He may or may not have preached on these texts
before, but most certainly the manuscripts were prepared during the last days of his last week on earth.
He always wrote the title and date on the outside of
the first leaf of his manuscript, and there is not
another mark on these but the titles and dates given
above.

Some time Saturday evening he wrote a brief
account of the proceedings of the week in his diary,
and ended with what he thought would be his work
next day: "Preached a.m. from Psalms cxix. 54,
and p.m. from 1 Peter i. 6."

But it is not given to any man to be able to write
his own diary in advance. The sermons were never
preached. That evening he took suddenly ill. His
physician, Dr. Philip, was summoned, and pronounced
the disease *angina pectoris*, a disease not necessarily fatal, but often so. Dr. Philip remained with
him a part of the night, and next day there were
symptoms of improvement. Everything that skill
and affection could do was done, and his friends
became quite hopeful. Monday he was so much
better that he dictated a number of letters for his
daughter Mary, who for years had helped him with
his correspondence. Towards evening he became

quite cheerful, and Mrs. Cochrane went out to make some arrangements about a marriage ceremony that he expected to perform next day. In the evening he rose for a moment and was again seized with intense pain. Dr. Philip was hastily summoned, but human aid was of no avail. At fifteen minutes after ten the call came. He slept quietly away. He "was not for God took him."

Eleven years before, when in poor health, he wrote in his diary, "Weak as I am, I keep at my desk when not on the sofa. I want to be found working when my Master comes." His prayer was literally answered.

It is difficult for people who do not know the position Dr. Cochrane occupied in Brantford to understand the shock his death gave to the community. He was one of Brantford's best known citizens. His figure had been familiar on the streets for thirty-six years. Everybody knew "the Doctor." He had preached in every pulpit accessible to a Presbyterian minister, and spoken on every platform. To the older citizens his voice was as familiar as their own. He had touched the community at many points.

The shock was all the greater, too, because nobody thought of Dr. Cochrane as an old man, or as a feeble man ; much less did they think of him as a dying man. He was so active, so energetic, so aggressive, so versatile, that his neighbours naturally looked upon him as the embodiment of life and activity. When his sudden death was made known the heart of the city was moved, and it seemed impossible for people to realize that Dr. Cochrane was no more.

Next day the daily press conveyed the sad intelligence to all parts of the country. People over all the Dominion learned with surprise and sorrow that one of the most active and aggressive ministers of the Gospel in Canada had passed away. To Presbyterians, especially, the bereavement was painful, and all the more so because wholly unexpected. Everybody knew that George Brown had been mortally wounded ; that Alexander Mackenzie's health was feeble ; that Sir John Macdonald was dangerously ill; but nobody outside of Brantford knew that Dr. Cochrane was not at work until they learned that he was dead.

Tuesday and Wednesday the body lay in state in the house on Charlotte Street that had been his home for years. His pulpit gown took the place of a shroud, and a bunch of heather from his native hills—the gift of one of the oldest members of Zion Church—lay at his head. The expression of the well-known face was calm and peaceful. At last rest had come. Many came to take their last look. Strong men could not restrain their tears as they passed the bier on which the body of their old friend and neighbour lay.

On the afternoon of Thursday the funeral took

ADAM SPENCE.

place, and was attended by many friends from a distance. A brief service was held in the house, conducted by Dr. Warden, assisted by Dr. Hamilton, of Motherwell, and Dr. Wardope, of Guelph.

In giving an account of the remaining services of that sad afternoon we condense from the excellent report of the Brantford *Expositor:*

"Shortly after two o'clock the cortege formed before the manse to proceed to the church. The pall-bearers were Messrs. George Watt, Charles Duncan, William Watt, sen., Adam Spence, Thomas McLean, William Grant, S. M. Thomson, and Dr. Nichol.

"As the long cortege moved off, the bell on the Congregational church, a stone's throw distant, pealed out in measured strokes, and the alarm bell at the fire hall joined in the solemn measure.

"The procession formed as follows :

Sons of Scotland.

Flower-Bearers.

Hearse.

Pall-Bearers.

Relatives and near friends.

Session and Managers of Zion Church.

Officers and Teachers of the Church and Mission Sabbath Schools.

Presbytery of Paris and attending Clergymen.

Brantford Ministerial Association,

Session and Managers of the First Presbyterian
Church.
City Council.
Board of Trade.
Collegiate and Public School Boards.
Public Library Board.
Board of Free Library Trustees.
Citizens' Carriages.

"AT THE CHURCH.

"The scene along the route and at the church
was a remarkable spectacle. Hundreds of citizens
thronged the streets and endeavoured to secure admission to the church. Long before the hour at
which the cortege was expected, the church was
crowded to repletion. The scene has seldom been
approached in Brantford. The interior of the church
was heavily draped in black. The entire front of the
pulpit was hidden in the sweeping folds of the same
material ; the pillars were covered, and around the
galleries the funereal draping was looped from point
to point. The bright spot in the church was the
communion table, which was laden with the flowers
brought from the house. The casket reposed on a
small platform just inside the altar, where a ray of
sunlight from the south window fell athwart the silver
plate.

"The first seven seats in the centre aisle were reserved for the mourners. In the pulpit sat Rev. G. C. Patterson, of Embro, Moderator of the Paris Presbytery, who presided ; Rev. Dr. Warden ; Rev. Dr. Torrance, Moderator of the General Assembly ; Rev. R. M. Hamilton, President Brantford Ministerial Association ; Rev. Dr. McMullen, of Woodstock, and others.

"The music for the service was particularly appropriate. The hymns were No. 198, 'In the Cross of Christ I Glory'; 346, 'The Sands of Time are Sinking'; and 328, 'Now the Labourer's Task is Over.'

"Rev. Mr. Patterson, of Embro, after the arrival of the funeral cortege at the church, addressed the immense congregation in very touching language.

"Mr. Patterson said : 'We are met in the shadow of a great sorrow, and our hearts go out to those who are so sorely stricken. He whose loss we mourn to-day was a man of broad and generous sympathies; a man of large and varied attainments ; a man of great capacity and power ; opportunities crowded upon him—opportunities for service—and through all these years, with untiring earnestness, he sought to make the very most of those opportunities. He occupied a very large place in the life and work of the Church. He stood in close relations with many interests and institutions in the city ; in closer relation still to this

Church. Many, many, in the days that are to come, as you look back and remember, will say :

> " Oh, for the touch of a banished hand,
> And the sound of a voice that is still."

" ' Many of you particularly who have known his great sympathy and his warm heart, and those of you who received your first impulse heavenward under his ministry, will realize the force of this truth. Who is there among men who can reckon up the results of such a ministry ? It is needless that I should say more, for there are those here, representing various interests and organizations, and the whole Church, who are to speak to us of him and of his work.'

" Rev. Mr. Cockburn, of Paris, then read portions of the fourth chapter of 1 Thessalonians and the seventh chapter of Revelation, after which

" REV. R. M. HAMILTON,

of the First Presbyterian Church, of Brantford, representing the Ministerial Association, alluded to the deceased pastor : ' My dear friends, it is my privilege, as President of the Alliance, to speak to you on their behalf this afternoon. I am sure that there is not a member of the Alliance who would not eagerly take my place, and perform this duty towards our most distinguished member. There are many among us who have known him longer than I have, and this would enable them to couch the eulogy in more graceful speech, but none feel more than I do upon what I am called upon to say on this occasion. The Alliance, along with other organizations which have always had the assistance of our father and brother, has suffered a severe loss. No figure will be so greatly missed from this Alliance ; our fellowship in the Alliance has been of the best and most profitable character. All Protestant denominations meet there in the most cordial sociability ; the most perfect freedom of speech is given, which means the most honest and candid expression of conviction, so that we have an opportunity of judging of one another's merits that is afforded in no other way. To a minister nothing is so dear as his religious convictions. In all these relations no one has been more staunch to his faith, and, at the same time, more liberal and kindly in his treatment of an opponent ; no one could more good-naturedly defend his position than the deceased, nor more kindly point out defects in others. It was due to his public spirit that the Alliance was organized many years ago, and in a material degree to his untiring interest in it that it has been maintained. Several times during the past twenty years it was wrecked, and each time Dr. Cochrane rallied the ministers of the city about him and re-established it.

Our gatherings, which were rather of a social nature, meeting from house to house, have been very frequently the recipients of the hospitality of his own home. Even when, by reason of sickness in the home where a meeting was to be held, or where some minister, from lack of sympathy, desired the meeting to be held in a church's parlors, the Doctor's home was open, the table spread, his genial wife just as cordially and generously assisting him. Our last meeting was at his home, and although his wife was attending at the bedside of her sister, we were once more made welcome under his hospitable roof, and although the table-talk was more subdued, still he was very genial.

" ' A MANY-SIDED MAN.

" ' He was a many-sided man, but no feature of his character was more noticeable than his sociability. His merry fund of stories always kept us in good humour. Notwithstanding his love of fun, he was never frivolous, nor did he ever descend to that unworthy platform called anecdotage. At social gatherings he was welcome in every church. He had the faculty of presenting the old Gospel truth in an interesting and practical manner, and seldom, or never, did he allow the opportunity to pass without bringing home some truth for this life or the life beyond. He retained the enthusiasm of youth to the very last. It was always the astonishment of his brethren that he was able to fill so many positions, and so well. He was a Christian minister, a genius in the Courts of the Church, with an influence wider than this broad Dominion, an active educationalist ; but, almost more than any minister we ever knew, a citizen. Nothing affecting the welfare of the community escaped his notice or lost his interest. I think I can safely say that the success of many of our manufacturers and business men is partly due to the unceasing interest he took in matters of a public nature. Notwithstanding his busy life, he never allowed a stranger to lack a greeting ; he was always the first to call upon a brother minister coming a stranger to Brantford, and when anyone left the Alliance he got proper credentials. We love to think of our dear father and brother who has so unexpectedly taken his departure from our midst. He has ceased his labours, and his works do follow him ; he has fought the good fight, he has finished his course, he has kept the faith, and he has received the crown of righteousness. He enjoyed many honours, wielded a large influence, and had a continental reputation. To-day he is with Christ, which is " far better."

"'THE ALLIANCE'S SORROW.

"' In concluding my remarks, let me express the deep sympathy of the Alliance with his stricken family—the widow and children. We commend them to the God of all comfort. A true husband and a kind father, his loss can only be endured by casting themselves upon the solace, mercy and providence of God. We sympathize with the congregation, whose heads are bowed in sorrow over the remains of a wise counsellor and a beloved and faithful friend. Those whose lives have been spent in united service under his leadership, you will never find another to take his place. The young will attach themselves to another pastor, but your loss is too great to be taken up by anyone else.

"' God's honoured servant has been taken away, for while "God removes the worker He carries on the work."

"' One word more—in regard to the cordial relations that have always existed between Dr. Cochrane and myself during the past four years that I have been associated with him in Brantford. Always happy in our intercourse, we have been frank-minded, and I shall not soon forget his kindness. The two churches have been drawing more closely together, and during the past two or three years the most kindly intercourse has been continued, and to-day we mourn him as one whom we love.'

"Dr. McMullen, the clerk of the Paris Presbytery, then delivered the following address, after being introduced by Rev. Mr. Patterson :

"' Christian Friends,—Any words which I can hope to command must be utterly inadequate to voice the feelings of the Presbytery, in whose behalf I am requested to say a few words, for the brethren would like to pay some seemly tribute to the name and memory of one whom they held in such high honour and affection. The people of Brantford, mourning to-day as I suppose they have never mourned over the loss of any citizen previously, can well understand what I mean when I say that Dr. Cochrane held a place in the hearts of his brethren altogether unique and special. He gave distinction and prominence and weight to our Presbytery among the Presbyteries of the Church, as all the ministers from other Presbyteries here present, and the venerable Moderator of the General Assembly will, I am sure, bear me witness. Dr. Cochrane's well-balanced judgment, his capability of taking a broad, common-sense, Christian view of any Church question, filled the brethren with confidence in his judgment, and seldom had we occasion to differ from the view which he had advocated or advised when we were taking counsel together in regard to any perplexing questions affecting the congregation, or the work of the Church in general.

"'A LEADER.

"'Constitutionally he was a leader among men. He could not be anything else. His energy and force of character were such as would necessarily bring him to the front anywhere, and he had a marvellous adaptability, such as that he could fill any one of a large number of positions and fill it with efficiency and success.

"'Then the large-hearted, generous good nature that always characterized him, fitted him peculiarly for smoothing over a difficulty when it arose, reconciling differences, and acting the part of the peacemaker, and thus leaving in harmony those who might be disposed to hold conflicting sentiments.

"'HIS ENERGY.

"'He was full of energy. I have often wondered, as his brethren have wondered, how he could endure the amount of work and the wear and tear which that amount of work involved. He was continually going hither and thither in connection with the work of the Church, and more particularly the Home Mission work of the Church, which held such a warm place in his regard.

"'For the past thirty-six years or more I have been

in intimate association with Dr. Cochrane, and oh, I can scarcely believe that I am at his funeral to-day—I can scarcely believe it—I cannot take in the thought, somehow, that he is gone, but so it is.'

"At this moment Dr. McMullen's feelings almost overcame him, and it was with great difficulty that he steadied his voice sufficiently to allow him to proceed. Many of the vast congregation were weeping, and the scene was very solemn and impressive indeed. Dr. McMullen continued :

"'During these past thirty-six years I have had many confidential conversations with Dr. Cochrane. I never heard him indicate that he felt any anxiety or worry about his own private or family affairs, never ; but I never met him that he was not talking about the work of the Church and anxious about it, and devising plans and methods by which that work might be carried on with greater efficiency and success. Oh, brethren, not even do I attempt, in the name of the Presbytery of Paris, to say what ought to be said in honour of the name and memory of him whom we all loved and honoured, for that worth of character which more and more we learned to appreciate.'

"REV. DR. TORRANCE,

the venerable Moderator of the Presbyterian Church in Canada, addressed the congregation. Dr. Torrance said :

"'Dear Christian Friends,—We are met to-day to speak of and mourn our loss. A home in Brantford has suffered a loss—the loss, as you have heard it stated, of a good husband and a kind father. This congregation has suffered a loss—the loss of a faithful, energetic pastor, who has long laboured among you in word and in doctrine. The Brantford Ministerial Association has suffered a loss—the loss of a much-loved friend and companion, a man of broad views, of cheery sentiment, of extensive hospitality. The institutions of education in Brantford have suffered a loss—especially let me refer to the Brantford Young Ladies' College, of which our departed friend and brother was governor, and long the presiding spirit and genius. And the City of Brantford has suffered a loss—of a citizen being taken away who had its interests deeply at heart. And, as you have just heard from my esteemed friend and brother, Dr. McMullen, the Presbytery of Paris has suffered a loss—one who was for years its clerk, and who handed over the burden of its duties to him who has so ably filled it, and up to the date of his death a member of that Presbytery ; and, as you have heard from Dr. McMullen, he stated in all his conversation how deeply the interests of the Church rested upon his heart, overtopping all personal and private considerations.

"'And the Synod of Hamilton and London has

suffered a loss, for the hand of its clerk lies now stiff under the power of death; no more shall that hand hold the pen to record on the pages the records of its proceedings, and no more shall the members of that Synod hear his voice, either pleading for, or resisting, measures or proposals that come up for consideration. And, my friends, the Presbyterian Church in Canada has suffered a loss—the loss of a man remarkable for his versatility and adaptability of those gifts and powers that the creating God had conferred upon him; the loss of a man who was fully consecrated to the Church's service; and the glory of the redeeming Head and Saviour has ever been promoted by that service. And it has lost a man who was doing more than any other two members of the Church; remarkable in watching for his opportunities, for discharging the duties laid upon him by the Church. Let me give you an incident of recent occurrence. Not long ago, cards were issued, calling a meeting of the Committee upon the Distribution of Probationers, in Hamilton, at 1 o'clock in the afternoon, Dr. Cochrane being a member of that committee. Just after these cards were mailed, there came an intimation from the Senate of Knox College, Toronto, that they were to have a meeting the same afternoon, in Knox College, and with the next mail I received from Dr. Cochrane a card, suggesting that the hour of the meeting of the

Distribution Committee should be changed to the forenoon. There was time to give notice of it. This was to enable both of us to attend the meeting of the Senate, as well as the other meeting; and, carrying out his suggestion, leaving my own home and he leaving his home at a somewhat similar hour, by early train, we held our meeting in the forenoon at Hamilton, did all the work of the Distribution Committee, took the train at Hamilton for Toronto, and spent four or five hours at the meeting of the Senate, in Toronto, at Knox College—an exemplification of the energy of the man, and the ability with which he could embrace opportunities.

"'The Church will suffer a great loss in the removal of Dr. Cochrane. He was Convener of the Home Mission Committee. My good brother, Dr. Warden, can speak of his energy and ability in the discharge of the duties of that most important committee.

"'I cannot tell you now for how many years—for more than a quarter of a century we have been associated together in the work of that committee; and in attending its meeting one was always struck with the method that displayed itself in his arrangements. All the business was brought forward in its proper order and place. One was struck also with the energy with which he presided over these meetings, continuing sometimes for a day; with the ability with which he grasped the subject which was brought before us, and the wisdom with which he pointed to certain conclusions and decisions; and then, again, those who are upon that committee will never forget the quickness with which he called to order, and with which he proposed a motion or amendment, when they were to be submitted to the committee, the speed with which the vote was taken, and the decision declared. These are facts that will long linger in the memory.

"'One was also struck at the ability to grasp the work as it came year after year upon his hands. Comparatively small in the years to which my memory looks back, the committee could then take in the work of supplemented congregations, and of assigning supplies to vacant charges. Then, again, we can never forget the fulness with which he brought forward the reports of that committee from year to year before the General Assembly. The "Blue Book" of the Presbyterian Church in Canada will be a memorial through many years of the industry, the skill, the ability of Dr. Cochrane, the Convener, and its compiler.

"'At the General Assembly, when Home Mission work came up for consideration, as that report was sketched, or its contents indicated to us, and as he threw himself with that fervour that you all know, have all seen, and have all felt its power, in upholding the interests of Home Mission work, stretching, as it were, from ocean to ocean, and through the length and breadth of Canada—yes, the Church has suffered a loss in the removal of the Convener of Home Missions from the work to which he had been so long devoted.

"'There is other work in connection with the Church from which he has been taken away, work which he faithfully discharged in his day and in his generation ; but, having served his generation, he has, by the will of God, fallen asleep.

"'Brethren, we speak of our loss. Natural that we should do so. It is, perhaps, the first thought that suggests itself to us in such circumstances as these ; but, oh, I often think, as I stand by the coffin of one who is asleep in Christ, that we are too selfish, that we make too much of ourselves, think and speak too much of our loss, and do not give that prominence that we ought to give to the gain of him whose loss we mourn. Our loss is his gain to an extent that we cannot comprehend.

"'We look this day upon the mortal remains, and for the last time, of a servant of God. No doubt many of you will pay a visit to the last resting place where his body will be laid ; dear ones of the family will often think of that spot, and often repair to it,

Let all look forward to that time when the resurrection trumpet shall sound, when this mortal shall have put on immortality, when death shall have been swallowed up in victory. We know what the corruptible body is; we do not know what that glorious body shall be, but it shall be made like unto Christ's own glorious body; and those eyes, now in the sleep of death, shall be opened to behold the King in His beauty, in His excellence and majesty.

"'My dear brethren, our loss is great. It is not all darkness; there is the light from afar, sufficient to cheer the heart in the sorrow through which we are now passing.'

"Dr. Torrance was followed by

REV. DR. WARDEN,

representing the Home Mission Committee.

"Dr. Warden said that in view of the number of addresses already made, and of the fact that many would like to take a last look at the deceased pastor, it would not be wise for him to make an address of any length. The Doctor continued: 'There lie the remains of the busiest and most active man I ever knew, and I think, with perfect truth, the epitaph can be inscribed on his gravestone: "Abundant in labours." Most of you are familiar with his labours as pastor of this congregation; many of you are familiar with the

12

work he accomplished in connection with the city of Brantford, not only in connection with the Ladies' College, of which he may well be said to have been the father, and the active governor during all the years of its history; with the interest he took in this community; with his work in connection with the Synod and this Presbytery; with his work in connection with the Church as a whole; his interest in General Assembly meetings, how prominent he was, and how efficient in conducting the work of the Assembly; with the work he rendered in connection with Knox College for so many years. Some few of us are familiar with the work he rendered in connection with the Presbyterian Alliance. One of his most effective services was in connection with the Home Mission Committee. He has occupied this position for, I think, twenty-six or twenty-seven years. I have been privileged to have been associated with him during twenty-six or twenty-seven years, and think I know him well, and I know I express the mind of every member of that committee when I say that, under God, to him largely the successes of our Church for the last twenty-five or thirty years have been due. There are few manses in Ontario, Quebec, the North-West Territories, and British Columbia, where the tidings of Dr. Cochrane's death will not come as tidings of the loss of a personal friend. It has been remarked this afternoon that he did as much as two men in connection with the work of the Church as a whole.

"'That is true. No man has done more to help the ministry of this Church to obtain positions, and to help them in these positions. He has been a friend of the ministers of our Church, and, as I have said, in the homes of many of these ministers and families to-day the tidings of his death come as the tidings of the loss of a personal friend.

"'When Dr. Cochrane became Convener of the Home Mission Committee there was little work to do. The work has rapidly grown, until there are upwards of four hundred missionaries in connection with our Home Mission field, and upwards of four hundred Home Mission stations that are supplied with Gospel ordinances by means of this Home Mission Committee. I would like to dwell upon how he will be missed by all the brethren who are in the habit of meeting from year to year, by all of whom he was looked upon as a warm friend. Last week he was in Toronto, apparently in his wonted health and strength, and, with the earnestness and vigour which characterized him, discharging his duties.'

"Dr. Warden then related how a young man who had led a wild life came in, after most of the members had left, and how Dr. Cochrane talked with him, and gave him a substantial contribution towards his passage to the North-West, where the young man wished to go, in order to break away from his associations.

"The speaker continued: 'I love to think of this incident, and will cherish it in my memory for years to come, as an incident in the last closing days of his life.

"'THE CALL TO WORK.

"'Brethren in the ministry, let me remind you, as I desire to be reminded myself, that the night cometh when no man can work. One by one, the friends with whom we have taken counsel together have been removed. Let us hear the call, more distinctly and emphatically than ever, "Work, work, while it is yet day."

"'Our hearts go out in tender, loving sympathy for those who have been bereaved. Let it be the earnest prayer to-night that the Husband of the widow and the Father of the fatherless may be found, in their blessed experience, "A very present help in time of need."

"'Our hearts go out in sympathy toward this congregation, who have lost their pastor. To-day, this one and that one said: Dr. Cochrane is woven into the very life of this household; he buried my father; he spoke the closing words to my mother in her last moments of life ; he baptized my children. We cannot think of Brantford, we cannot think of the congregation of Zion Church, and really feel that we have lost our minister.'

" The congregation were almost unable to restrain their emotion at these touching words, and many of of those present wept bitterly.

" Dr. Warden concluded by appealing to them to let the truth which Dr. Cochrane had endeavoured to proclaim sink into their hearts and minds ; that the dead pastor would have no stronger desire, could he look down upon his people, than that those who have not already accepted Christ should accept Him upon this the day of his funeral.

" A LAST LOOK.

" The people then passed along and took a last look at the deceased pastor. It took upwards of half an hour for the grief-stricken procession to pass, not only those in the church, but the hundreds outside, who could not gain admittance, being permitted to view the remains. The manifestations of grief were most affecting, and the scene one of an almost heart-rending character.

" On leaving the church the cortege proceeded to Greenwood to consummate the last sad exercises. Hundreds of citizens lined George Street to the cemetery as the solemn procession wound its way toward the city of the dead.

" The Cochrane plot at Greenwood is located on the western side of the little gore in the centre of the grounds. It is marked by a single shaft of marble, and just to the left the grave was prepared. The earth heaped upon one side was covered with emerald green cedar sprouts.

" Several hundred citizens watched the proceedings, which were of a simple nature. The shell and casket were lowered, and the gathering stood with bared heads while the Rev. Dr. Robertson lifted his voice in an impressive appeal to the Almighty. This concluded the exercises, and the flowers were reverently placed about the mound while the crowd slowly left the cemetery."

As the people slowly leave, can we lay a more beautiful flower on his grave than the following editorial from a little paper published by the Mission Band of his own church :

"Once more our little paper has resumed publication. We are glad we are back again to hard, earnest work for the great cause of missions. But our gladness is overshadowed by a great sorrow, for we write over our editorial column ' In Memoriam.' To-day we are mourning one who has gone to a land from whence none ever return. The words we could utter in his praise would be weak and faltering compared to his merits, nor are they necessary after the eloquent and glowing tributes paid our beloved dead by his brother ministers; but we can drop the sweet flower of remembrance on a grave that will ever be green in our memory. As yet we seem not to realize that he is gone; but in the days and weeks that are to come, when others preach from that pulpit where for so many years he pleaded the cause of Christ's kingdom, when we miss from our streets the small, energetic form of the man who lived every hour of his life to the fullest, then our souls will cry out in Tennyson's immortal words, 'Oh for the touch of a vanished hand, and the sound of a voice that is still!' He has gone; but has left behind him such a ' footprint on the sands of time,' that, come what may, it will never be effaced.

" Hush ! the Dead March wails on the people's ear ;
 The dark crowd moves, and there are sobs and tears,
 The black earth yawns, the mortal disappears.
 Ashes to ashes, dust to dust, —
 He is gone, who seemed so great.
 Gone ! but nothing can bereave him
 Of the force he made his own ;
 Being here, and we believe him
 Something far advanced in state,
 And that he wears a truer crown
 Than any wreath that man can weave.

> Speak no more of his renown,
> Lay your earthly fancies down.
> And in the vast cathedral leave him ;
> God accept him, Christ receive him."

This editorial was sent to Mrs. Cochrane by Miss Eleanor Duncan, Superintendent of the Mission Band. In her most appropriate letter, Miss Duncan says : " What will we do without him ? is the cry of every heart." No grave divine, no newspaper expert described the feeling in Zion Church better than it was described by Miss Duncan in this short sentence : "WHAT CAN WE DO WITHOUT HIM? IS THE CRY OF EVERY HEART."

Our Heavenly Father dealt kindly with Dr. Cochrane in many things. His business training in Paisley was no small part of the equipment that made him so useful in after life. Than Mr. Robert Brown, of Cincinnati, no struggling student ever had a more generous friend. The little Scotch Church in Jersey City was a good congregation to begin with. The pastor was not overburdened with work, and his mind was quickened by contact with the pulpit of the great city of New York. Brantford was a good field of labour in every way, and Zion Church was as worthy a congregation as any pastor could desire. In all these things and in many more Dr. Cochrane was highly favoured, but in nothing was God's kindness

more wonderfully displayed than in the time and manner of His servant's death. He could not have carried his burden of work much longer, and lessening it in any way would have been to him a sore trial. To see another preacher in the pulpit of Zion Church, to see another pastor going out and in among the families he had visited so long, to see another Convener presiding over the Home Mission Committee, and another official in charge of the College—to see all this would have darkened his closing years. To him retirement would have been existence, not life. It is not given to many strong men to be able to retire gracefully and allow others to do the work they used to do. God spared Dr. Cochrane the ordeal. The Master called him in the midst of work. He had not to resign anything. He fell at the head of his column with all his armour on.

And God's kindness, too, was strikingly displayed in the manner of his death. To " take farewell," as he himself used to phrase it, was a much more serious matter for Dr. Cochrane than it is for most men. He seldom left a place that he liked without wondering whether he would see it again, or said good-bye to a friend who lived at a distance without thinking they might never meet again. Parting from a member of his family for a few weeks was a sore trial, and sometimes brought the tears. To have said his long farewell to his weeping wife and children as they stood around his death-bed would have been a greater trial for him than death itself. God saved him from that trial, the last that could come. All that a kind husband and a good father could say had been said many times. There was nothing more to be said, nothing more to be done, and God quietly took His servant home.

Dr. Cochrane left a widow and four children. William, his eldest son, is Bursar in the Institute for the Deaf and Dumb in Belleville. Miss Cochrane resides in Pomfret Centre, Connecticut.

His twin sons, Alexander Robertson and Robert Balmer Brown, are attending the Toronto University. Mrs. Cochrane is now a resident of Toronto. Few people have been called upon to suffer so much in so short a time. The death of her sister, her husband, and her father, and the breaking up of her home in Brantford, all came within a few months. All was borne with a Christian fortitude that no words can describe. Many of the best people of the Presbyterian Church, no doubt, remembered her in their best moments.

CHAPTER IX.

In Memoriam—Telegrams, letters and resolutions of condolence—Memorial sermon by Dr. McMullen—Reminiscences by Professor Bryce and Dr. McMullen.

ABOUT three hundred letters and telegrams of condolence were received by Mrs. Cochrane within a few days of her husband's death. They were sent from Scotland, from the United States, and from all parts of Canada. To publish all in this volume is, of course, an impossibility. A selection has been made, mainly according to the locality in which the letters were written, the object being to show how widespread was the sorrow caused by Dr. Cochrane's death. And let the reader remember that this man, about whom these letters were written and these resolutions passed, came to Canada a perfect stranger thirty-six years ago. Perhaps his only friend in Canada, at that time, was Dr. John Thomson, of Galt, and Dr. Thomson left soon after Dr. Cochrane's arrival. Presbyterians have a constitutional process by which they ascertain what is "the mind of the Church." This chapter is an expression of the heart of the Church, and the heart of the Church is quite as important as its mind.

THE LATE PRINCIPAL KING.

Mrs. (Dr.) Cochrane :

Much sympathy.   Sorry distance prevents attendance at Dr. Cochrane's funeral.

John M. King.

DR. A. M. STEWART, *Scottish-American*, NEW YORK.

Mrs. (Dr.) Cochrane :

The sincere sympathy of my wife and myself goes to you and your family in your great bereavement.

A. M. Stewart.

PROFESSOR BRYCE, WINNIPEG.

Mrs. Cochrane :

Accept our warmest sympathy in your great trial.

Geo. Bryce.

DR. CAMPBELL, Moderator of the General Assembly.

Sheriff Watt :

Please express to Mrs. Cochrane and other members of family my sympathy with them in their bereavement. May God sustain and comfort them these sad days.

R. Campbell.

HON. A. S. HARDY.

Sheriff Watt:

Please say to Mrs. Cochrane how deeply Mrs. Hardy and I deplore the irreparable loss, and sympathize with her in her overwhelming affliction. The loss is not hers alone but the entire country's, and, even more notably, that of Brantford. Truly a great man has fallen. I trust to be able to be at the funeral.

A. S. Hardy.

DR. TORRANCE, Ex-Moderator of Assembly.

Accept deep and sincere sympathy from Mrs. Torrance and myself.

Robt. Torrance.

DR. ROBERTSON, Superintendent of Missions, Manitoba and the North-West.

Mrs. Cochrane:

May God sustain you and yours in the sudden and severe affliction that has overtaken you. Sorrow here is general and profound.

J. Robertson.

DR. WARDEN.

Mrs. (Dr.) Cochrane:

My heart feels sore for you all. May God abundantly comfort you.

Robt. H. Warden.

MR. DANIEL WATERS, son of the late Dr. Waters.

Mrs. Cochrane :

We read with sorrow the notice this morning of your sudden bereavement. You have our heartfelt sympathy.

Daniel Waters.

REV. A. MCLEAN, BLYTH.

Sorry cannot attend funeral. Deep sympathy of Mrs. McLean and myself.

A. McLean.

REV. NEIL MCPHERSON, HAMILTON.

Kindly accept my heartfelt sympathy in your sudden and sore bereavement.

Neil McPherson.

REV. JAMES ROBERTSON, QUEBEC.

Deeply sorry to hear of your loss. All here sincerely sympathize with you in your bereavement. Will write.

Jas. Robertson.

PRESBYTERY OF TORONTO.

At Toronto, and within Knox Church there, on Tuesday, 1st November, 1898, the Toronto Presbytery met at ten o'clock in the morning.

Inter alia—A committee consisting of the Rev. Dr

Warden, Rev. Dr. Gregg and Rev. Mr. Jordan, was appointed to prepare a minute anent the death of the late Dr. Cochrane.

The following is the minute submitted by the Committee, which it is agreed to forward a copy of to Mrs. Cochrane :

In view of the recent death of the Rev. William Cochrane, D.D., of Brantford, Convener of the Home Mission Committee of the Presbyterian Church in Canada (Western Section), the Presbytery of Toronto agreed to place on record an expression of the high respect and esteem with which they regarded him.

Without referring particularly to the multitudinous and valuable services which, during his remarkably busy life, Dr. Cochrane was enabled to render as a minister of the Gospel, as a member, clerk and Moderator of the various courts of the Church, as President of the Presbyterian Ladies' College, and as taking part in other important spheres of labour, the Presbytery would especially refer to his great work as Convener of the Home Mission Committee (Western Section). For this position he was singularly gifted with executive ability, and in the discharge of its duties his labours were abundant, energetic and unwearied. During the many years of his convenership there has been marvellous progress in the Home Mission operations of the Church.

Hundreds of mission stations have been established, and these have grown into congregations, the congregations into Presbyteries, and the Presbyteries into

Synods. This progress has been in a large measure due, under God, to the indefatigable services of Dr. Cochrane. He now rests from his labours on earth. The Master has called him to enter into rest, and he has doubtless received the glad welcome, " Well done, good and faithful servant, enter thou into the joy of thy Lord."

With the bereaved partner of his life, and the other members of the family, the Presbytery deeply sympathize in their great affliction. May the God of all consolation be their Comforter in all their trials, and bestow upon them all the blessings they need for time and for eternity.

In name and on behalf of the Presbytery of Toronto.

Robert H. Warden,
Convener of Committee.

PRESBYTERY OF PARIS.

Minutes of the Presbytery of Paris on the death of Dr. Cochrane, adopted December 13th, 1898.

Dr. McMullen, Convener of the Committee to prepare a suitable minute on the death of Dr. Cochrane, submitted the following, which, on motion of Dr. McKay, seconded by Mr. Leslie, was adopted :

With a sense of loss and a feeling of sorrow which words cannot adequately express, the Presbytery of Paris records the death of the Rev. William Cochrane, M.A., D.D., beloved pastor of Zion Church, Brantford, for thirty-six years, who departed this life October 17th, 1898, in the sixty-eighth year of his life, and the fortieth year of his ministry, having been ordained and inducted into his first pastoral charge in Jersey City, United States, June 7th, 1859, and translated to Zion Church, Brantford, May 14th, 1862.

His noble qualities of character, exceptional adaptability, distinguished gifts, untiring industry, and abounding labour, together with his ready and forcible eloquence on the platform and in the pulpit, and his consecration of heart and life to the service of Christ, made him a man of power, and won for him the love and admiration of his brethren. In addition to his labours as pastor of a very large and growing congregation, he discharged with marked efficiency the duties of Clerk of this Presbytery for fourteen years, and the duties of Clerk of the Synod of Hamilton and London from the date of its formation to the time of his death.

He was mainly instrumental in founding the Brantford Ladies' College ,and held the office of Governor of that institution.

By annual appointment of the General Assembly, he held the office of Convener of the Home Mission Committee of the Presbyterian Church in Canada for over twenty-six years ; and in 1882 the Church conferred on him the highest honour in her gift by investing him with the office of Moderator of the General Assembly, which met that year in St. John. On the day of his funeral, business was suspended in the city of Brantford, and a vast concourse of people assembled in and round Zion Church, in which a solemn and appropriate service was held, conducted by the Rev. G. C. Patterson, Moderator of Presbytery, assisted by Rev. R. M. Hamilton, Rev. Dr. McMullen, Rev. Dr. Warden, Rev. E. Cockburn, Rev. Dr. McLaren, and the Rev. the Moderator of the General Assembly, Dr. Torrance, of Guelph, and Rev. Dr. Robertson, Superintendent of Home Missions, who offered prayer at the grave.

On the following Sabbath memorial services were held in Zion Church conducted by Dr. McMullen, assisted in the evening by Mr. Hamilton, minister of First Church, both the congregations uniting in the service, and the Elders of both occupying the front pews.

The foregoing brief and imperfect recital of facts and circumstances connected with the life and death of our beloved and honoured brother appears to us the most appropriate and forcible testimony of the noble character of the man, and the high esteem and affection in which he was held by his brethren in the Presbytery and throughout the whole Church.

To his bereaved widow and family the Presbytery extend assurances of deep and tender sympathy, as also to his warmly attached and sorrowing congregation, and pray that the God of all grace and comfort may sustain them in their sore trial.

G. S. Patterson,

Moderator.

W. T. McMullen,

Clerk.

PRESBYTERY OF GUELPH.

At Guelph, and within Knox Church, the fifteenth day of November, one thousand eight hundred and ninety-eight, the Presbytery of Guelph met and was constituted *sederunt*, Mr. Thomas Wardrope, D.D., Moderator *pro tem.*, etc.

Inter alia—The following resolution, submitted by the Rev. Dr. Torrance, was unanimously adopted, and the clerk was instructed to forward a copy to the family of the late Dr. Cochrane:

The Presbytery of Guelph, having had its attention called to the sudden and unexpected death of the Rev. William Cochrane, D.D., of Zion Church, Brantford, would record with solemn feelings its sense of the loss that has thus been entailed, not only on the bereaved family and the congregation to which he so long and faithfully ministered in holy things, but on the Presbyterian Church in all parts of Canada, on a large circle of friends and acquaintances to whom he was personally known, and on a still larger one to whom he was known only by reputation.

Coming to Canada in the vigour of his manhood, he devoted himself to the interests of the pastoral charge to which he had been called, and had the gratification of seeing the work of the Lord prosper among his people till the day he fell asleep, having served his generation by the will of God. Possessed of great versatility of talent, and characterized by great activity of energy, he cheerfully accepted opportunities of usefulness that presented themselves out-side of his pastoral labours ; and special mention may be made of his connection with the Home Mission work of the Church in the Western Section of the Dominion, which he saw grow from small beginnings to the large proportions which distinguish it at the present time, and which afford promise of still greater increase as our population swells in numbers and the resources of our congregations are developed and more fully consecrated to the service of Christ.

Of him it must be testified that he was abundant in labours, instant in season and out of season, kind and charitable in his disposition, and ready to place his services at the disposal of any in all cases in which he thought he could be instrumental in pro-moting the glory of God.

The prayer of the Presbytery is that those who knew his work best and who feel his loss most, may have seasonable and sufficient grace for their support, guidance, comfort and profiting.

Extracted from the Records of the Presbytery of Guelph.

Robert Torrance,
Presbytery Clerk.

Guelph, 17th Nov., 1898.

PRESBYTERY OF WHITBY.

The Presbytery of Whitby, in session in Oshawa, on Tuesday, October 18th, desire to express their deepest sympathy with the family of the late Rev. William Cochrane, D.D., in their sudden bereavement.

We are conscious of the loss sustained by the Presbyterian Church at large in the death of one who was conversant with every department of the Church's work. We find it hard to realize that Dr. Cochrane's voice will be heard no more in our Church Courts, and that his seat will be vacant at the Home Mission Board, with which he has been so long associated.

While mourning the loss that will be felt throughout our whole Church and country, we would not forget the family circle so sorely tried, and would most respectfully tender to you assurance of our sympathy and tears and prayers.

Extracted from the scroll minutes of the Presbytery of Whitby this 20th day of October, A.D. 1898.

J. McMechan,

Presbytery Clerk.

Port Perry, Oct. 20th, 1898.

PRESBYTERY OF STRATFORD.

To Mrs. Dr. Cochrane and family :

Dear Mrs. Cochrane,—The following is a resolution of the Presbytery of Stratford in reference to the decease of your late lamented husband :

Inter alia—It was moved by Dr. Hamilton, seconded by Mr. Panton, that :

" The Presbytery of Stratford embraces this opportunity, at its first meeting since the lamented death of the late William Cochrane, D.D., of Brantford, to record its deep sense of the loss which the Presbyterian Church in Canada has sustained in his decease.

In addition to his faithful pastoral work as a minister of a large congregation for thirty-six years, he has been the energetic Convener of the Home Mission Committee of our Church for twenty-six years; the duties of which office he discharged with great devotion and ability, which contributed greatly to the success of the Home Mission work of the Church.

"The Presbytery would unite with many others who personally know Dr. Cochrane, in expressing deep sympathy for his widow and family, and pray that they may always be sustained by the gracious promise of our Heavenly Father."

The resolution was unanimously carried and the Clerk requested to transmit a copy to yourself and family.   I am, faithfully yours,

J. D. Fergusson,
Clerk of Presbytery.

PRESBYTERY OF VICTORIA.

The Presbytery of Victoria hereby embraces the first opportunity of placing on record its sense of the loss which the Church at large has sustained in the lamented death of the Rev. William Cochrane, D.D., of Brantford, Ontario, Convener of the General Assembly's Home Mission Committee.

To his mature judgment and indefatigable energy must be credited, in no small measure, the present position of the Presbyterian Church in Western Canada. His visit to the Pacific Coast, some fifteen or sixteen years ago, prepared the way for taking over, by the Canadian Church, of the work that hitherto had been carried on by the Church of Scotland, and led to the more aggressive prosecution of the work throughout the whole Province.

To the congregation of Zion Church, Brantford, and to the members of Dr. Cochrane's family, we beg to tender our respectful sympathy.

D. MacRae,
Clerk of Presbytery of Victoria.

Mrs. Cochrane;
  The Manse, Zion Church,
    Brantford, Ont.

PRESBYTERY OF LONDON.

The following minute was adopted by the London Presbytery, at the November meeting, relative to the death of Dr. Cochrane, of Brantford :

The Presbytery took note of the death, on the 17th October last, of William Cochrane, Doctor of Divinity, for thirty-six years, and at the time of his death, minister of Zion Church, Brantford, in the Presbytery of Paris. The Presbytery recognizes with great sorrow and solemnity the suddenness of his summons to the presence of the Master whom he served, and the greatness of the loss which the whole Church has sustained, especially in connection with Home Mission work, the Convenership of which he held with great energy, zeal and efficiency, ever since the union of the Churches in 1875.

The Presbytery earnestly prays, and cherishes the

faith, that the great exalted Head of the Church will raise up other faithful men to fill with efficiency the places He is, in His inscrutable providence, causing from time to time to be vacated, and that He will grant special guidance to the Church at this particular juncture.

The Presbytery express their sympathy with the bereaved widow and children, and pray that the God of all grace, who comforteth those that are cast down, may support and cheer them with the consolations of the Spirit, which are neither few nor small.

George Sutherland,
Clerk.

Fingal, 9th Dec., 1898.

Presbytery of Renfrew.

Minute of the Presbytery of Lanark and Renfrew anent the death of Rev. Dr. Cochrane :

The Presbytery records its sense of the great loss which the Church has sustained in the death of the Rev. Dr. Cochrane, for so many years Convener of the Assembly's Home Mission Committee, and an active and earnest leader in all branches of the Church's work.

In this Presbytery, where so large a work has been done under the care of the Home Mission Committee, we know much of his earnestness and very much of his kindly and sympathetic nature. He was our friend always, and with the whole Church we shall long cherish the memory of the enthusiastic, loving-hearted and devoted leader, whom in the very midst of abundant labours the Master has called to his rest and reward.

We tender our sympathy to the grief-stricken family of our Brother, and commend them to the consolation and care and grace of Him who is able to comfort in any trouble, and whose righteousness is to children's children of them that fear Him and keep His covenant.

John Crombie,
Clerk.

Smith's Falls, 26th Nov., 1898.

Presbytery of Chatham.

Resolution of Chatham Presbytery regarding the death of the Rev. Dr. Cochrane :

The Presbytery desires to take this earliest opportunity of placing on record its sense of the great loss which the Church has sustained in the sudden death of the Rev. Dr. Cochrane, of Brantford.

By reason of his broad sympathies, his deep humanity, and the varied public activities with which he was associated, Dr. Cochrane was much more than a parish minister. He belonged to the entire Presbyterian Church in Canada ; and the phenomenal energy and capacity for work which he manifested for so many years as Convener of the Home Mission Committee, and Superintendent of the Ladies' College, placed almost every section of Western Canada under tribute to him as a personal benefactor. Judged by the volume of his labours, his unfailing responsiveness to the many obligations of life, and his conspicuous ability in the discharge of duty, he occupied a rank which is equalled by few. Most royally did he establish his worthiness to the many honours which the Church bestowed upon him. While grateful to God for a life which was so full of labour, the Presbytery expresses its deep regret that so faithful and able a servant of God has gone from its midst, and also desires to convey to the bereaved widow and the members of the family its sincere sympathy with them in these hours of their sorrow.

Extracted from the minutes of the Presbytery of Chatham.

W. M. Fleming,
Clerk.

Essex, Ont, 20th Dec., 1898.

DELIVERANCE OF THE PRESBYTERY OF HURON *re* DR. COCHRANE'S DEATH:

The Presbytery of Huron desires to place on record its high esteem for the late Rev. William Cochrane, D.D., of Zion Church, Brantford, whose unexpected death came as a shock to his numerous friends. By his removal the Presbyterian Church, who now deeply mourns his loss, is deprived of one of her foremost ministers. In labours more abundant, instant in season and out of season, with a marvellous capacity for work, which he exerted to its fullest extent not only in his own congregation, but also in the duties entrusted to him by the courts of the Church, especially in connection with the Assembly's Home Mission Committee, of which he had been the untiring Convener for many years, Dr. Cochrane has left behind him a noble record. This Presbytery, while mourning his loss, would thank the Head of the Church for the high order of talents which He bestowed on His servant, and which were so fully consecrated to his Master's cause. Finally, the Presbytery wishes to convey to Mrs. Cochrane and the other members of the family its deep sympathy with them in their great sorrow, and prays that they may be comforted by Him who, because He Himself hath suffered, being tempted, is able to succour them that are tempted.

On behalf of the Presbytery,
Arch. McLean,
Presbytery Clerk.

Blyth, December 6th, 1898.

HOME MISSION COMMITTEE, PRESBYTERY OF BARRIE.

Barrie, November 1st, 1898.

Mrs. (Dr.) Cochrane, Brantford :

Dear Madam,—At a meeting of the Executive Committee on Home Missions of the Presbytery of Barrie, held this forenoon, advantage was taken of the first opportunity afforded to refer to the decease of your late husband, the Rev. Dr. Cochrane. I was instructed to acquaint you of the sorrow and surprise with which the brethren learned that he was taken away. They shared in the high regard in which he was held throughout the Church, and beyond it, on account of his gifts, his various labour and service to the cause of religion so diligently performed till almost the last day of his life on the earth. They desire to express sympathy with you in your bereavement, and respectfully express the hope that you may partake of divine consolations, believing that he, though removed from his earthly home, is with Him who is the Life indeed.

I am, dear madam,

Yours respectfully,

Rob. Moodie,

Convener of the H. M. Committee of Presbytery of Barrie.

PRESBYTERY OF OTTAWA.

Wakefield, Que., November 16th, 1898.

Dear Mrs. Cochrane,—I beg leave to send you the following resolution, which, at the last meeting of the Presbytery of Ottawa, was moved by Rev. Dr. Armstrong, seconded by Rev. Dr. Moore, and carried by a standing vote :

" That this Presbytery place on record its deep sorrow at the sudden death of Rev. Dr. Cochrane, Convener of the Assembly's Home Mission Committee, and its appreciation of the indefatigable earnestness and consummate ability with which he discharged every duty laid upon him by the Church.

"The Presbytery would convey to Mrs. Cochrane and family its deep sympathy with them in the sudden and sore bereavement that has visited them, and pray that the Father of mercies and God of all comfort would visit them with His divine consolations."

Believe me,

Very sincerely yours,

R. Gamble,

Clerk of Presbytery.

SYNOD OF BRITISH COLUMBIA.

The Home Mission Committee of the Synod of British Columbia embraces the earliest opportunity of placing on record its sense of the loss sustained by the Church in the death of the Rev. Dr. Cochrane.

By his versatility, capacity for business, eloquence as a preacher, and aptitude for public affairs, he rendered valuable service to the Church and community.

For over a quarter of a century he presided over the Home Mission Committee of the General Assembly, helped to shapen its policy and guide its work, and had the satisfaction of seeing Synods and Presbyteries organized where only feeble stations and struggling missions were found a few years ago.

The Committee would express its sincere sympathy with his widow and children in their sorrow, and would commend them to Him who has promised to be a present help to His people in their time of need.

SESSION OF THE FIRST PRESBYTERIAN CHURCH, BRANTFORD.

Brantford, October 28th, 1898.

Dear Mrs. Cochrane,—Under instruction from the Session of the First Church, the following resolution of sympathy is addressed to you, which we trust you will accept as only a slight expression of our sympathy for you and your family in your present sore bereavement :

" The session of the First Church desires to express to Mrs. Cochrane and the members of her family sincere sympathy in their sore affliction. While the Church and society at large will miss Dr. Cochrane much, the blank left in his home is infinitely greater. His genial manner, good judgment and wise counsel, apart from the memory of the past, are no longer at their command, but may the God who is made unto us wisdom, and righteousness, and sanctification, and redemption, make up what is lacking to them in the day of sorrow, and may the glorious hope of the resurrection comfort all their hearts in the day of trouble."

R. M. Hamilton,
Moderator.

A. J. Cromar,
Clerk.

SESSION AND BOARD OF MANAGEMENT OF ZION CHURCH.

The members of Session and Board of Management of Zion Church, in this dark day of their history, desire to express to Mrs. Cochrane and family their profound sorrow at the sudden and unexpected death of their beloved pastor. While more particularly interested in his labours in Zion Church, we gratefully recognize the honour he has conferred upon us in the various important positions he occupied in connection with the Presbyterian Church in Canada. Possessing splendid executive abilities, few ministers within its bounds did so much for the Church as a whole, but he never allowed the numerous calls on his time to interfere with the discharge of his duties as pastor of Zion Church. To say that everyone of the eight hundred members of Zion Church loved Dr. Cochrane would not all express the intensity of their affection for him. We can never forget his tireless energy, his ceaseless attention to the sick and the unfortunate, and the warm-hearted sympathy so generously extended to all in need; nor can we forget the irresistible power of the impassioned eloquence that thrilled our souls as from the pulpit he proclaimed the Gospel of the Christ he loved so well. We thank God that a man endowed with talents and gifts so rare was given to Zion Church, and that for thirty-six years of harmony and peace he remained its pastor, during which period of time he was ably and lovingly assisted in various forms, socially and otherwise, by Mrs. Cochrane and his affectionate daughter. To Mrs. Cochrane, Miss Cochrane and the other members of the family the loss is irreparable and sad beyond expression. We earnestly pray that He who was the guiding star of the husband, father and pastor so dearly loved by all—the Great Head of the Church—may pour into their hearts that comfort and consolation which He alone can give, and that, cheered on by the sure and certain hope of a glorious immortality, they may be strengthened patiently to endure this sore trial, "ever looking for that blessed hope and the glorious appearing of the Great God and our Saviour Jesus Christ."

Signed on behalf of the Board of Management,

William Watt, sen.,

Chairman.

Signed on behalf of the Session,

Thomas McLean,

Clerk.

In no part of the Dominion was the good influence of Dr. Cochrane's work as Convener of the Home Mission Committee more felt than in the Synod of Manitoba and the North-West Provinces. The Home Mission Committee of the Synod passed the following resolution, which speaks for itself:

The Committee embraces this, its first opportunity, of placing on record its appreciation of the great loss sustained by Home Missions, and Christian work generally, by the death of the Rev. William Cochrane, D.D. For more than a quarter of a century he was elected, by successive Assemblies, as Convener of the Home Mission Committee of the Western Section; and the rapid progress made by the Presbyterian Church, especially in the new Western Canada, is in no small measure due to his sympathy and guidance.

WILLIAM WATT, SEN.

The rapid extension of work demanded a buoyant revenue, and his eloquent advocacy and untiring energy helped greatly to place the need before the Church and to secure the requisite means. His most enduring monument is the large number of strong churches, nursed as missions and developed into congregations, that are to-day doing so much to extend the Kingdom of Christ at home and abroad.

The Committee desires to express its sincere sympathy with Mrs. Cochrane and all the members of the family, who have been so suddenly and sorely bereaved, and commends them to the loving care of our Father in heaven.

The Committee over which Dr. Cochrane so long presided passed the following :

The Home Mission Committee (Western Section) would hereby place upon record its sense of the loss sustained in the death of the Rev. Wm. Cochrane, D.D., for over twenty-six years its honoured Convener.

During all those years his interest never flagged and his energy never tired. Advancing years neither dulled the edge of his enthusiasm nor weakened his courage in facing an ever-enlarging field for work. The success which has attended our work of Church extension owed not a little to his large outlook, his wise guidance, and his hopeful advocacy of the claims of the newer districts. As its head, he won, and kept to the end, the love and confidence of the members of the Committee. By his death we have lost a co-labourer beloved, the Home Mission fields and missionaries a sympathetic friend, and the whole Church an enthusiastic advocate ; her Home Mission work one whose eloquent appeals bore fruit not only at home, but awakened interest and called forth help from the sister Churches in the Motherland.

It was characteristic of his whole life that his last public work should be that of planning enlarged spiritual help to the miners in the mountains. May his removal in the very midst of his efforts for more effective work in the distant parts of our land be an incentive, not only to every member of the Home Mission Committee, but also to every member of our Church.

The Committee tenders its heartfelt sympathy to Mrs. Cochrane and the family in the sore affliction which has befallen them, and commends them to "the Father of mercies and the God of all comfort, who comforteth us in all our affliction."

FROM THE SYNOD OF HAMILTON AND LONDON.

Dr. Thompson reported for the Committee appointed to prepare a minute regarding Dr. Cochrane, late clerk of the Synod, which was adopted, ordered to be entered in the minutes and a copy sent to Mrs. Cochrane. It is as follows :

The Synod desires to put on record its sense of the great loss which it has sustained since its last meeting in the removal by death of our venerable and venerated brother, Dr. Cochrane, whose works of faith and love in the Church have been so abundant and so varied.

Ever since the formation of this Synod, at the time of the union of the Churches, Dr. Cochrane has performed the duties of Clerk, extending over a period of twenty-four years, and during all this time he commended himself to the most exacting judgment of the brethren, and was among them all " a brother beloved."

Further, this Synod hereby expresses its appreciation of the great and unceasing services which Dr. Cochrane was enabled to render the whole Church of which for thirty-six years he was a cherished member, and a most faithful minister of the Gospel, and one who endeared himself, not only to his own ever increasing flock, who now fondly cherish his memory, but to the Church at large which he served so long and faithfully.

Our departed brother had many and rare gifts which fitted him for a many-sided service in the Gospel ministry, and all of which he used without stint and to the utmost of human possibility. His influence has been felt in every department of the Church's work and throughout the bounds of the Dominion. He has put the whole Church under a debt of gratitude to the Master who gave us His servant to labour so faithfully in His vineyard.

The Synod would make special mention of his invaluable services in connection with our Home

Mission work, of whose committee he was the trusted Convener for twenty-six years. Here he showed a devotion seldom known among men, for his interest, instead of flagging, grew in intensity with the growth of years.

His brotherly disposition and genial manner, so free and lively and unrestrained, endeared him to all to whom he ever stood in any relation.

We thank God for the distinguished place He was pleased to give our brother in the Church, the rare endowments with which he was blessed, which made him a guide and a leader in our Church Courts, and one who helped to shape her policy.

We feel that our brother has left us, who yet serve in the ministry, a singularly noble example of devotion to duty, of untiring industry, of loyalty to the Church of which he was an ornament, as well as his deep and abiding interest in those other questions that concern the welfare of our country, and in all the institutions of our land that have for their object the welfare of our fellowmen. As a citizen and a patriot, no less than as a churchman, we may well copy his life. . We pray for a baptism into his spirit of self-forgetful devotion and zeal in all noble works, and for efficiency in the Gospel ministry, and that the Lord of the vineyard may raise up other labourers into the harvest.

***

SYNOD OF MANITOBA.

It was agreed, on motion of Rev. Dr. King, seconded by Rev. Dr. Bryce, that the Synod of Manitoba and the North-West Territories desires to record its deep sense of the loss sustained by the Church through the unexpected removal by death of the Rev. Dr. Cochrane, of Brantford, Ont.

The Synod desires to express its high appreciation of the value of the services rendered by him to the Home Mission work of the Church, and especially to that portion of it embraced within the bounds of this Synod, during the long period in which Dr. Cochrane acted as the energetic and untiring Convener of the Assembly's Home Mission Committee.

The Synod would also express its deep sympathy with his widow and family in their bereavement, and desires to commend them to Him who is the God of all comfort.

Extracted from the records of the Synod of Manitoba and the North-West Territories by

S. C. Murray,

Synod Clerk.

Port Arthur, Ont., November 14th, 1898.

The Augmentation Committee, for years closely allied with the Committee on Home Missions, expressed their appreciation of Dr. Cochrane's labours as follows :

The Committee record their sense of the great loss which has befallen the Church and the cause of missions through the death of Rev. Dr. Cochrane, so long the Convener of the Assembly's Home Mission

Committee, and also of the Augmentation Sub-Committee during the twelve years of their joint working. To few men has it been permitted to do so much work in laying broad and deep foundations on which is being reared a superstructure beneficial alike to Church and State. How energetically and how wisely he guided the work, we can all testify—sparing himself in nothing that the ever-increasing demands of the field under his supervision required of him. Still, with armour on, he heard the Master's call to enter into rest and reward. We shall miss him much, and would be reminded to be working " while it is day, for the night cometh when no man can work."

To Mrs. Cochrane and the bereaved family we extend sympathy, and our prayer is that God, whose righteousness is unto children's children, may watch over them for good, and guide and keep them in all their ways.

———

Resolutions of condolence were also passed by the following bodies :

The Municipal Council of the city of Brantford.

The Brantford Board of Trade.

The Brantford Public School Board.

The Collegiate Institute Board of Brantford.

The Ministerial Alliance of Brantford.

The teachers and pupils of the Brantford Young Ladies' College.

The Directors of the Young Ladies' College.

The Society of Christian Endeavour, Zion Church.

The principal, officers and pupils of the Ontario Institute for the Blind.

The Committee on Distribution (Western Section), Presbyterian Church.

The Board of the Brantford Free Library.

The St. Andrew's Society of Brantford.

The Camp Scotia, Sons of Scotland, Brantford.

---

218 South Broadway,

Los Angeles, October 24th, 1898.

To Mrs. (Dr.) Cochrane, Brantford, Ont., Canada :

My Dear Mrs. Cochrane,—This morning I was taken by surprise, on receiving a Canadian paper, to find the sad news of the loss of your dear, good husband.

In my house he was esteemed as a brother, and with his bright, cheerful manner had a hearty welcome at all times. His kind, loving disposition endeared him to many hearts, and he will be greatly missed, not only as a fond husband and father, but throughout the Church, to whom he gave his life-work.

He has gone home to his reward, where some of us are looking forward soon to meet him.

Dear Mrs. Cochrane, you and your family have my deepest sympathy, such as I have not words to express.   May a loving Saviour bless, comfort and support you in this great trial, is the prayer of

Your sincere friend,

D. Galbraith.

———

Toronto, Oct. 22, 1898.

Dear Mrs. Cochrane:

I was very sorry I was in Kingston when the telegram went to Toronto.

I need not tell you how shocked I was when I saw my dear friend's death in the paper.   I cannot think it possible he is gone.   The Church will miss his great services to a degree we can hardly realize—until his energetic presence is felt to be away from the great Christian enterprises in which he took such an illustrious part.

You have my deepest sympathy in your loss.   I know full well what such an experience as you are called to undergo means.   The only help in such cases is the Saviour Himself.   And He does come near to us when deep troubles overtake us.   No doubt this is one reason why He afflicts us in life. The human stay is often removed to induce us to find the rich blessings of the Divine stay, as we are urged to lean more exclusively upon it.

Your dear husband died in the harness.   Is it not better?   True, the suddenness of such a death as his is trying to friends left behind, but I believe it is a blessing to those prepared to go.

Give my warmest sympathy to the family, and accept the same also for yourself, and believe me,

Yours most sincerely,

G. M. Milligan.

The Manse, Dundas, Oct. 20, 1898.

My Dear Mrs. Cochrane :

I sent you no telegraphic message of condolence, nor did I think it safe yesterday for me to attend the funeral of my dear, well-loved friend and brother. I am, however, happy to know that my presence was not needed, or perhaps my absence noted, amid the sad scenes of grief and sorrow which testified to the high respect in which your dear husband was universally and deservedly held.

But though absent in body, I was present in spirit yesterday, and my prayer for you and the other members of the family ascended to God. Perhaps this note, though late, may be not less welcome among the many that are pouring in on you. May God sustain and comfort you. So he is gone, and we shall never again meet in Assembly, Synod and committee : I feel the loss. I had no prospect, in one sense, of *working* with him again ; but I never thought that I should survive him. We have seen little of each other of late years ; but the memory of earlier years is fresh and pleasant to me. My first acquaintance with him was by letter in 1861, when he did me a great kindness in obtaining the release of one of my Cobourg people who foolishly enlisted in the Northern army. After the Union in 1861 we were thrown together in Home Mission work. Waters, King, Thornton, Inglis, etc., were our associates ; of these, King alone survives. In 1872 he took my place as Convener, just as the great work in the west was opening up.   He filled his office efficiently, and, assisted by Dr. Warden, Macdonnell, Campbell, etc., carried the work on with great success.   Our meetings at those times were helpful as well as pleasant, and many a kindness I received from my dear friend.

Ten years ago I asked him to come down for my fifteenth anniversary.   This he could not do.   In two weeks my twenty-fifth anniversary is to be held, and I had thought of him again, if his many engagements would permit.   It cannot be, however—for him it is far better.   Little did I think, when dear Waters was taken, that you would so soon have to mourn with his wife.   Your husband wrote me not long ago—last February—that the Church business had not now the interest for him that it once had, because so many were no more there.   I have been gradually removed from prominence in Church Courts, college, and public duties; but he was called while yet full of energy.   I knew he was failing, but never thought of heart disease.   The blow must have come on you with terrific, stunning force—most unexpectedly. God's will be done.   I will not give advice; I am sure you are finding consolation in God, and His grace will be sufficient.   Your happy life with him must be gratifying in review; but I know that even the remembrance of all he was to you, of all the work he did so well, and of all the honour and respect that were accorded him, cannot assuage the painful feeling of loneliness that fills a widow's heart.   I commend you to Him who is the husband of such mourners.

Please assure Miss Cochrane and her brothers of my deep sympathy, and believe me,

Yours truly and gratefully,

John Laing.

———

Vancouver, B.C., October 20th, 1898.

Dear Mrs. Cochrane :

I write to express the surprise and pain with which we have learned of your husband's death. How sudden it seems, and how strange !

I need not assure you that out here in the far West he will be as greatly missed as in the East, that was more particularly the scene of his untiring labours.

Neither need I tell you that you and those you love will have, in this season of darkness and bereavement, the prayerful sympathy of many, in all parts of the Church, who are personally unknown to you, but who knew and esteemed him whom God has called to the higher services of the Upper Sanctuary. May God abundantly comfort you all in this sore trial.

With deepest sympathy, in which Mrs. McLaren joins,   Believe me,

Yours very sincerely,

E. D. McLaren.

———

Mount Pleasant, Paisley,
November 10th, 1898.

My dear Mrs. Cochrane:

I write you with deep sympathy under your great loss and affliction.   The news of the death of your dear husband, my old and valued friend, which I saw announced in the head lines, I felt as a sudden bereavement. His was a life of rare energy, usefulness, and devotion to higher duty, and few can fill his place in any of the spheres he served, and your loss and Mary's is irreparable. You have much consolation in his memory ; he has been taken full of labours, honour and love. I trust you will be greatly strengthened at this trying time, and may your boys follow a father's steps in the Christian course and give you much joy in your future. Mrs. McGowan was here the other day, and she told me of Dr. Cochrane's kind letter to her. The end seems to have come not without some foreshadows of weakness. He rests now who seldom rested from hard work, and his works follow him. All here who knew him feel that the Church and every good cause has lost a friend and champion. I think, also, I have heard of another loss and sorrow in your circle. These are deep waters, but One is with His people as they pass through them. May He be with you and all yours—all who have lost a father and friend. Kindly remember me in her sad hour to Miss Cochrane, who I see was able to be with her father when departing. My daughter joins with me in all kind regards and sympathy. We may not again meet here, but may we all meet whither those we loved have gone before us.

My dear Mrs. Cochrane,
Ever sincerely yours,
George C. Hutton.

Office of the *Scottish-American.*
New York, October 26th, 1898.

Dear Mrs. Cochrane :

Last week I sent you a telegram, and also a copy of my paper, but I have felt unable to write to you until now.   The sad news was a great surprise to both Mrs. Stewart and myself.   We often thought of you last week, and the great loss you had met with.   I hope you have kept pretty well in health, and able to be about the house, at least.

I should have been to the funeral, but I was unfortunately situated here, and I could not leave the city. Mrs. Stewart was in bed, and one of my chief assistants broke down and was away from the office.   My work is so exacting that I cannot leave it at times.

The obituary in the *Scottish-American* was carefully prepared, and was my tribute to one I greatly loved, and a dear friend for almost forty years.   I feel his loss very keenly, and will miss his visits greatly. It was fortunate that he was here this last summer, and that I was able to see so much of him,

Mrs. Stewart is better now, and unites with me in sending kindest regards to yourself, Mary, and the boys.				Sincerely yours,

A. M. Stewart.

Toronto, October 19th, 1898.

My Dear Mrs. Cochrane :

It was a great shock to me when tidings of the Doctor's death was seen in the paper.   He seemed to me so active and vigorous that I never dreamed he would depart so suddenly. I sympathize with you and your stricken family most tenderly, and Mrs. Parsons sends her sympathy and love in this most trying hour. May the Lord comfort you in the " blessed hope." I regret very much that I cannot be present at the funeral services on Thursday, on account of the meeting of the Toronto Presbytery the same hour. Your honoured husband has borne so nobly the heat and burden of the aggressive work of the Church, that his name is almost a household word. He will be greatly lamented and greatly missed.

With great respect and sincere condolence in your very great bereavement, I am, dear Mrs. Cochrane,

Very sincerely yours,

Henry M. Parsons.

To Mrs. William Cochrane.

———

Montreal, October 18th, 1898.

Dear Mrs. Cochrane :

I was extremely shocked, on taking up the papers this morning, to read of the sudden death of Dr. Cochrane, and I beg to offer you my most sincere condolence and sympathy in your sad affliction. I am sure the news will be a terrible shock, not only to the members and congregation of Zion Church, where he so long and ably ministered, and to which he was so unselfishly devoted, but to the Church throughout Canada, and to everyone who has had the privilege of meeting him. May He whose faithful servant he was be with you in your sad affliction, and help you to bear it. Yours sincerely,

J. Elmsly.

Bank of British North America.

————

Brockville, October 19th, 1898.

My Dear Mrs. Cochrane :

It was with a feeling of sadness and sorrow that I read the announcement, per telegram, yesterday of the Doctor's sudden death. I was, and have been, one of his many ardent admirers for a number of years ; therefore permit me through this medium to extend to yourself and family my most sincere and heartfelt sympathy in your sad bereavement.

Believe me,

Yours most sincerely,

George A. Dana.

Mrs. Cochrane, Brantford. ·

————

Knox College, Toronto,

October 18th, 1898.

Dear Mrs. Cochrane :

I desire to express my very deep sympathy with you and the members of your family in the great sorrow which has so suddenly fallen upon you. Having heard nothing of Dr. Cochrane's illness, our surprise and sadness were great when we saw this morning that he had passed from earth. May you and your dear children be sustained by the Heavenly Comforter under this weighty stroke. Many will sorrow with you for one who was beloved of his brethren, and who delighted to help and comfort others. It is difficult to realize the fact that he whom we saw but yesterday so full of life and energy, in the midst of abundant labours, is to be with us here no more. But the work which he was honoured to do for his Master will live after him, and will be remembered always by those who saw or shared his labours. With what zeal and devotion he engaged in the several departments of service with which he was occupied, and especially in the great work of Home Missions! It will always be a comfort to you to remember the part which was performed by your admirable husband in organizing the Home Mission work of the Presbyterian Church, and thus in sending the ordinances of religion to large numbers who would otherwise have been without them. He must often have been exhausted and depressed (though he never seemed so) with his unceasing activities. But now his Lord has given him rest. He has not withdrawn him from service, but rather called him to service in which there is no fatigue and no pain. You will find great comfort in the thought that he has reached the land where there is no sorrow, and where all that he prayed for and aspired after on his own account has been realized. To be with Christ is far better.

The gracious Master will Himself be with you ; and you will look forward—even in your sorrow—to the time of blessed reunion.

May we all, through the infinite mercy of God and

the mediation of our Saviour, at length reach the home prepared for those who have loved and served the Lord.

Yours, with much sympathy,

Wm. Caven.

Tannachy Cottage, Orillia,

October 18th, 1898.

Dear Mrs. Cochrane :

I presume to intrude into your chamber of sorrow, and to express to you my very profound grief at the unlooked for death of your husband, as well as my deepest sympathy with you in the sad bereavement which has so unexpectedly come upon you.

We have been for a good many years the Senior Synod Clerks of the Presbyterian Church in Canada, and were some years ago thrown a good deal together, in connection with the Home Mission work of the Church.

In this, and in other ways, I became aware of the valuable public services which your late husband rendered to the cause of Home Missions. With this great and glorious work his name will ever be associated in the history of our Church.

His readiness, his intense earnestness, his versatility, and his power of adapting himself to all kinds of Church work, his herculean labours, and his burning zeal—one and all co-operate in making a blank in our Church life and work which it will be difficult to fill.

But the Lord, having use for him in the Church above, has issued his command, " Come up higher."

15

" Well done, good and faithful servant, enter thou into the joy of thy Lord."

I regret that the illness of my wife prevents me from attending the funeral of our dear departed friend.

Again tendering you my warmest sympathies, and praying that the Man of Sorrows may encircle you with His eternal arms, and give you, what He only can give, effectual comfort and support.

I am,

Yours sincerely and sympathetically,

John Gray.

Mrs. (Dr.) Cochrane, Brantford, Ont.

———

278 O'Connor St., Ottawa, Ont.,

October 20th, 1898.

Dear Mrs. Cochrane:

I cannot describe the feelings of surprise and sorrow which took hold of me when on Tuesday last, while waiting in the station at Smith's Falls, I read the announcement of Dr. Cochrane's death.

It will soon be thirty-six years since I first met Dr. Cochrane in the house of the Rev. Dr. Burns, then Professor of Church History in Knox College. Only last June, at the General Assembly, he and I were speaking of the conversation we had that night. During all these years the acquaintance then so happily begun has been to me a source of great satisfaction. It has been my privilege to work with Dr. Cochrane in many ways, upon matters which have had an important bearing upon the welfare of the

Church, and it gives me great pleasure to say that his unfailing cheerfulness and urbanity combined with his skill in affairs to make him not only a trusted, but a greatly beloved, leader among his brethren.

His abundant labours for many years past have been an astonishment to all.   I cannot resist the feeling that his zeal for the Church may possibly have shortened his days.   Of one thing I am sure, and that is that so long as the fruits of his labour remain, and they must remain while the Presbyterian Church in Canada continues to exist, his name must be held in grateful remembrance.   I beg to assure you and all his family of my deep sympathy in your affliction, and pray the God of all comfort to visit you all with those divine consolations which He only can give.

I am, sincerely yours,

Wm. Moore.

107 St. Anne Street, Quebec, P.Q.,
Tuesday, October 18th, 1898.

Dear Mrs. Cochrane :

The news of your dear husband's sudden taking away by the hand of death from the scenes of his earthly labours, reached us early this morning. Even prior to the receipt of Mr. Watt's telegram we had read in the morning paper a brief announcement of the sad event.

It is needless to say that we were all very much surprised by the suddenness of the stroke, and rendered deeply sorrowful, with a sense of great personal loss, by the death of one who was so dear a friend to each member of this household. Both of my sisters and my brother join me in expression of deepest regret for your bereavement, and in sincerest sympathy with you and with your family in this time of your sorrow and affliction.

Rev. Mr. Love, of St. Andrew's Church, came over from the Manse in the early morning, as soon as he heard the news, to express his sympathy and to speak his regard for him whose abundant life and labour had so endeared him to all his brethren in the ministry.

For myself, more especially, who was so long and closely intimate with him during all the twelve years of my ministry in Paris, I may say that he was to me as a brother tried and true, ever willing to help, ready to respond to every call; his joy " to spend and be spent in the Master's work," and when trial and affliction came he showed himself a friend indeed —one whose memory can never be forgotten.

And now his home, his congregation, his city, the whole Church in the Dominion, mourn his loss. More than any one I know, or have ever known, he was animated with the spirit of Paul, " diligent in business, fervent in spirit, serving the Lord," and the care of all the churches was upon him. Earth seems poorer because of his taking away, though heaven be richer ; and we, who are left mourning and desolate, journey on, trusting that in some brighter sphere we shall see again his cheerful presence and hear his welcome greeting.

His end was doubtless such as he himself would have desired, could he have chosen it. He died working, labouring and thoughtful for others unto the last, and then the Master's call came, " Come up higher," and the blessed commendation falls sweetly on our ears, " Well done, good and faithful servant, enter thou into the joy of thy Lord." And in our inmost hearts we respond, " Amen, and amen."

I have many pleasant remembrances of our meetings in later years. His gracious, kindly welcome to myself at your home in Brantford, in October, 1895; his visit here on his way back from Halifax, in the summer of 1897 ; our unexpected meeting in October last in New York City, and, lastly, his presence at the Assembly in June, in the city of Montreal—all these times are full of pleasant memories, and there is not the shadow of a cloud between.

I am leaving for Montreal this week. I intended to have gone last week, but was persuaded to defer my going, and now I am glad that I am here to write this letter of sympathy from the home where he was always so welcome a guest.

I am sure Miss Mary, as well as yourself, will feel the loss very deeply. I grieve with you both, and pray that the God of all consolation may comfort your hearts and minds with that comfort that he alone is able to impart.

Again with kindest regards to each and all the members of your household, and with all good wishes from my sisters, and my brother and myself, believe me,   Yours very faithfully,

James Robertson.

Toronto, October 19th, 1898.

Dear Mrs. Cochrane :

As one who had the honour of Dr. Cochrane's friendship, and who loved him, as all his friends did, permit me to express to yourself and family the sincere sympathy I feel with you in your sudden and sore bereavement. Mrs. Bengough, whose friendship with your sisters gives her an interest in you and yours, joins me in this expression. May God comfort you all.

Very truly yours,

J. W. Bengough.

---

77 Peel Street, Brantford, Ont.,

October 25th, 1898.

Dear Mrs. Cochrane :

By the strictest orders of Dr. Digby all news was kept from me, more especially anything calculated to excite or agitate me, hence it was not until very recently that I heard of your very sad bereavement, and of the loss we all sustain in the death of Dr. Cochrane. Permit me to assure you of the profound sympathy of one to whom he was ever a very kind friend. I was deeply touched to hear that almost the last time he was in his own pulpit, he was kind enough even to remember me in his supplication to the Almighty, praying for my restoration to health.

We may truly say of him that " he kept the whiteness of his soul, and thus men o'er men wept."

I shall ever regard him as the noble hero, who on the field of battle, in the glorious time of victory, in the hour of his most splendid triumph, yields up his life in the cause to which he had ever devoted it.

Pardon these lines if they seem an intrusion, but to be altogether silent seemed to me to be treating his past kindnesses and friendship and his incalculable worth with dumb forgetfulness, hence the first thing I essay to do is to pen these lines.

Believe me,

Yours most respectfully,

W. Raymond.

Queen's University, Kingston, Canada,

October 19th, 1898.

My Dear Mrs. Cochrane :

In common with the whole Church, I am profoundly grieved at the great loss which we—you most of all—have sustained. An engagement here prevents my going to you now, but I have asked Dr. Smith to represent the University. In the meantime accept my loving sympathy and prayer that our heavenly Father may comfort you in your sorrow. Ever, my dear friend,

Your affectionate friend,

Geo. M. Grant.

Castlehead, Paisley, 7th Nov., 1898.

Dear Mrs. Cochrane :

I was very much stunned on hearing of the death of your dear husband, and have scarcely been able to get the sad tidings out of my head since. At my advanced age, and being troubled with giddiness, it is rather an effort for me to write now ; but I felt constrained to express to you, for myself and my wife, our sincere sympathy with you on the loss of your gifted and loving, as well as much beloved, partner in life's journey. We were amongst his oldest friends now remaining in this old town of Paisley, and ever took a kindly interest in his ministerial career and his family relationship. I understand he was taken away very suddenly from the duties of his very active life, so that it can be said of him that he died in harness. The last message I had from him was a paper containing an account of his last visit to New York—his was, indeed, a busy life. Human sympathy is not of much avail to sorrowing hearts, yet it is grateful to our feelings, and we offer you ours in all sincerity in this the time of your sore trial. May our great High Priest, now passed into the heavens, abundantly comfort you and yours in this the time of your sad bereavement, and may rich supplies of Divine grace, which your worthy husband so long and so faithfully proclaimed, be found amply sufficient in this the time of your deep sorrow—so that when afflictions abound, consolations may much more abound.

Again assuring you of genuine sympathy from Mrs. Dobie and myself with you and your family I am, dear Mrs. Cochrane,

Your sincere friend,

Geo. Dobie.

106 Crescent Street, Montreal,
Oct. 24th, 1898.

Dear Mrs. Cochrane :

There are occasions when words utterly fail to express the thoughts that are uppermost in our mind. The death of your beloved husband, announced so unexpectedly, has occasioned profound sorrow throughout the length and breadth of the Dominion, but it is those who knew him best that have now the greatest difficulty in realizing the extent of the loss which the Church at large has sustained by his removal. The Church has indeed good reason to mourn his death, for no individual minister, so far as I know, has ever done more, nor so much, to advance her interests as Dr. Cochrane. During all the years of his residence in Canada, his time and his talents and his best energies were ungrudgingly placed at the disposal of the Church, and, on looking back over this long period of ministerial activity, it is pleasant to reflect that his work was eminently successful and highly appreciated, and now that he has been called to higher service we can but thank God for his faithful and useful ministry.

While joining with others in the general tribute of respect that is being paid to his memory, let me assure you of my warmest personal sympathy with you and your family in this the hour of your deepest sorrow. Your great loss has been his gain. Having finished his course, the good and faithful servant has entered into the joy of his Lord.

Commending you to the God of all true comfort

and consolation, who is able and willing to help us in every time of need, believe me,

Yours very sincerely,

James Croil.

———

Dominion Methodist Church,
Ottawa, Oct., 19th, 1898.

Mrs. Wm. Cochrane, Brantford:

Dear Mrs. Cochrane,—I cannot refrain from expressing the surprise and sorrow which Mrs. Rose and I felt last evening, when we read of Dr. Cochrane's sudden death. Your good husband was one of the very first to welcome me to Brantford twelve years ago, and since then I have been glad to speak of him as one of my honoured acquaintances. Brantford can never be the same city without him.

Doubtless the Saviour, whom he preached so faithfully for so many years, will sustain and comfort you and yours; and you may safely count on the sympathy of thousands of hearts.

With much sympathy, ever yours,

S. P. Rose.

———

Hamilton, Oct. 18th, 1898.

My Dear Mrs. Cochrane:

It is with sincere sorrow that I learn this morning of the unexpected death of your dear husband. Little did I think when I saw him last, so active and so full of interest in the work of our Church, that he would be so soon called away from us to his rest and reward.   He will be greatly missed by us in our Church work.   He served his blessed Master and the Church with great fidelity, energy and unwearied industry.   We will hold his name in grateful remembrance.   Mrs. Fletcher joins me in expressing to you sincere sympathy with yourself and the children in your sore bereavement.   May the God of all grace, in whose service the dear one who is gone laboured so faithfully, sustain and comfort you in this very trying affliction.

Sympathizing deeply with you, dear Mrs. Cochrane,
I remain, yours sincerely,

D. H. Fletcher.

Mrs. Cochrane,
The Manse, Brantford.

———

Oakville, Ont., Oct. 20th, 1898.

Dear Mrs. Cochrane :

On behalf of Mrs. MacBeth and myself, as well as on behalf of the family here, I wish to convey to you our deepest and truest sympathy in the great sorrow through which you have been called to pass.   Mrs. Patterson and I hoped to be able to attend the funeral yesterday, but circumstances prevented, and I spent an hour with your parents instead.   They all feel the trial keenly, though I know that your father, from his intimate acquaintance with the work of the Church, realizes more than any how much your husband's presence and activity will be missed by the whole Canadian Church.   It is now nearly twenty-five years since I saw Dr. Cochrane first in my father's house at Kildonan, on the Red River, and ever since that time your husband has been the steadfast friend and champion of the great Home Mission field which was just then coming into notice. Verily, a great man has fallen in Israel.

Only the other day I walked with him up Yonge Street, Toronto, to Dr. Warden's office, and, though he was bright as of yore, I realized that his abundant labours were beginning to tell upon him. The last time he was in Winnipeg (1897) he preached for me in the morning, in the presence of a great congregation, from the words of Christ, " I am come that they might have life, and have it more abundantly," and people felt that it was one of his greatest sermons. The memory of his abundant work and his untiring devotion will remain as a precious legacy to the Presbyterian Church, and we pray that the God of the fatherless and the widow will comfort and guide those into whose sacred sorrow we cannot fully enter.

Your very sincerely,
R. G. MacBeth,
(Of Winnipeg).

Hamilton, Oct. 18th, 1898.

Dear Mrs. Cochrane :

We were all, as was the Church and the country, very much shocked this morning on learning of the sudden death of Dr. Cochrane. For him we can only be glad, for to " depart and be with Christ is far better," but for you and your family it is very sad. I understand, too, that you lost your sister in death very recently. You have my deepest sympathy in your heavy and sore sorrow. If it can be any comfort to you, you can be assured that in a very real sense all the Church is mourning with you all. Only a month ago I sat with him on the Committee on Distribution of Probationers, which met here. I feel personally bereaved. I shall never cease to remember him with deepest gratitude for all his kind attention to mother and sisters during their residence in Brantford, and especially to Miss Jane during her long illness. He was kindness itself embodied. Everyone who knew him would concur in this.

There is so much I might write, but I shall not weary you. May the God of all comfort, to whom your beloved has gone, minister to you and yours all comfort in Christ Jesus, in the day of your great sorrow. Should the funeral be on Thursday, as is probable, I regret much to say I shall be unable to be present. Only public duty will keep me away.

With sincerest sympathy,

I am yours truly,

J. G. Shearer.

Montreal, October 19th, 1898.

Dear Mrs. Cochrane :

We were all startled to see a paragraph in the papers last night announcing the sudden decease of my good friend, your husband. You will have many communications of all kinds, no doubt, pouring in upon you ; yet I cannot forbear, seeing how much I have been associated for many years past with Dr. Cochrane ecclesiastically, troubling you and intruding upon your sorrow with a word of sympathy. Startling though the event has been, it is the ideal termination to a life such as your husband led. He died at his post, as every hero ought. Death came not to him as a surprise for, doubtless, with the apostle, "he died daily." Its suddenness could not dismay a heart firmly resting on the Rock. The secret of his energy and activity was the trust he had in his Redeemer. It was this that made his strenuous life possible ; and now he has entered upon his rest and reward. This will be your comfort, and a vast comfort it is, along with the prospective reunion, to be consummated in the Lord's good time.

Giving loving sympathy to Miss Cochrane and the young gentlemen ; and believe me,

Yours in Christian hope,

Robert Campbell.

Mrs. Cochrane,
  The Manse, Brantford.

———

340 Wood Ave., Montreal,
October 18th, 1898.

My Dear Mrs. Cochrane :

I was deeply shocked this morning to learn from our local paper of the great and sudden loss you have sustained. Dr. Cochrane was one of the oldest friends I had in the world, and although the distance by which we were separated has prevented us from meeting so often as I should have liked, yet a meeting was always to me a delightful revival of old friendship. I retain a specially pleasing reminiscence of the evening I spent in your house the last time I was in Brantford. It is a great gratification to me as an old friend, and of course it is a deeper gratification to you, to reflect on the long career of active service which has been granted him in the cause of the Master.

My son, who now occupies an excellent position in Montreal, and is living quite near us, will, equally with his wife, be deeply grieved over your great sorrow.

Be assured, my dear Mrs. Cochrane, of my sincere sympathy with you and your family in this sore bereavement, and believe me,

Very truly yours,
J. Clark Murray.

Barrie, Oct. 21st, 1898.

Dear Mrs. Cochrane :

I desire to express to you, along with the whole Church, my deep sorrow at the departure from our midst of your beloved and revered husband, Dr. Cochrane.

The tidings of his death came with a great shock to me when I took up the paper yesterday on the train, coming home from a visit in the States. Had I learned of it in time I would like to have gone and joined the friends in their last tribute of esteem and affection at his funeral. I trust that the universal sympathy manifested to you and the family, as well as the consoling thoughts arising from his life of usefulness and honour, may sustain you in this hour, and that our Heavenly Father may comfort you under your sore bereavement. It was a great pleasure to me to meet with the Doctor at last Assembly, where he displayed his usual vigour and ability in all his work.

He appeared to have lost none of his energy and to be as untiring as usual in his labours. His death is a great loss to the Church and to the country, but into your feelings none can enter but the Divine Consoler himself. The affection with which his memory is cherished must ever, in your great sorrow, afford you very precious comfort, and you may be assured that the prayers of many will be offered up for yourself and family at this time.

Mrs. McLeod joins with me in kindest regards and sincere sympathy.   I am,

Yours fraternally,
D. D. McLeod.

———

London, October 20th, 1898.

My Dear Mrs. Cochrane:

It is a very difficult task for me to undertake to write what is called a letter of condolence to you at this time. It is only because I feel it impossible for me to refrain from uttering a word of sympathy for you, however useless it may be in this the time of your great loss. There will be much said and written to you about Dr. Cochrane's eminently useful life, and of the high esteem in which he was held by the Church and the country at large. However grateful you may be to remember this at another time, just now your thought will be that your husband is taken from you, and that your children have lost their father. There is only one Comforter, and that is the Christ who said: "I am the resurrection and the life." I intended to write you a note of sympathy on the loss of your sister, Mrs. Watt, and now this heavier blow has fallen.

"Blessed be the God and Father of our Lord Jesus Christ, the Father of mercies and God of all comfort, who comforteth us in all our affliction, that we may be able to comfort them that are in any affliction, through the comfort wherewith we ourselves are comforted of God."

I am sure that your faith in God and in His Son Jesus Christ will sustain you. I am sorry that, owing to a previously made engagement, I am not able to attend the funeral service.

Will you kindly convey assurance of my sympathy to Miss Mary and the boys, as well as to your parents and sisters in their sad loss.

With sincerest sympathy,
I am, very truly yours,
W. J. Clark.

———

Woodstock, October 18th, 1898.

Dear Mrs. Cochrane :

I don't know what to say, or how to say it. Oh, so sudden! I am overwhelmed. I knew Dr. Cochrane

16

for a quarter of a century, and I hope I am a better Christian because of his acquaintanceship. The Lord be with you in this dark hour.

I expect, of course, to attend the funeral.

Yours, in profound sympathy,

W. A. MacKay.

MEMORIAL SERMON, PREACHED BY DR. McMUL-
LEN IN ZION CHURCH, BRANTFORD, THE SAB-
BATH AFTER THE DEATH OF DR. COCHRANE.

"And Hezekiah slept with his fathers, and they buried him in the chiefest of the sepulchres of the sons of David ; and all Judah and the inhabitants of Jerusalem did him honour at his death."—2 Chronicles xxxii. 33.

What a mystery is death! What a mystery is life! We see the signs and manifestations of life in the plant, the tree, the man; but the entity called life, the thing itself, no human eye has ever seen— something that eludes our keenest vision leaves the plant, the tree, the man; the visible and familiar form remains, but the form is dead. We stand by the coffin of a departed friend to take the parting look at the familiar face. All that our eye beheld is there; but the real personality—that, like its invisible Crea- tor, we never saw—is gone! The spirit has returned to God who gave it. Death spares not even the most useful and honoured life. Death entered the palace of King Hezekiah, filled it with gloom and sorrow, left the throne vacant, and filled the nation with grief and lamentation.

He was one of the reforming kings of Judah; he put down idolatry and restored the worship of the true God. He called an assembly of the priests and Levites, and addressed them on the importance of their sacred duties to the Church and nation; he set them to work to cleanse and purify the temple, and get things in order for the service and honour of God, and the good of the people.

He sent invitations to the piously inclined in the sister kingdom of Israel to unite with the people of Judah in a great Passover at Jerusalem. Many accepted the invitation. And as everything could not be got in readiness for observing the Passover in the first month, the fixed and proper time, the king and his princes took counsel to hold it in the second month, and the king prayed for the people, saying : " The good Lord pardon everyone that prepareth his heart to seek God, the Lord God of his fathers, though he be not cleansed according to the purification of the sanctuary. And the Lord hearkened to Hezekiah and healed the people."—2 Chron. xxx. 18-20.

Having filled the throne of the kingdom of Judah with great success and honour for twenty-nine years,

"Hezekiah slept with his fathers, and they buried him in the chiefest of the sepulchres of the sons of David; and all Judah and the inhabitants of Jerusalem did him honour at his death."

With the recollection of Dr. Cochrane's vast and impressive funeral in my mind, coupled with the memory of his eminently useful and honoured life, this epitaph of King Hezekiah has occurred to me as a fitting text for this memorial service. For a prince and a great man has fallen in Israel.

And now, what are some of the reflections suggested by the text and this solemn occasion with which we are connecting it?

1. There are some people who charge that this is a cold, unappreciative and ungrateful world in which we live; that its best benefactors have been ungratefully used, and that there is much in it to sour a man's heart against it, and to chill the sympathies of even the person of noblest and most generous nature; that philanthropic efforts to lighten the burdens and mitigate the hardships of the great mass of humanity have been thwarted by cold indifference on the part of those whom it was sought to benefit, and that therefore such efforts have largely failed of their object.

True it is that prophets, apostles, martyrs and witnesses for the truth are entitled to rank in the forefront among the very best friends humanity has ever had ; and yet they all met with cold indifference or hostility on the part of those whose good they sought. Of a greater than any of them, " the Friend that sticketh closer than a brother," it is written: " He came unto his own, and his own received him not." By the hands of wicked men he was crucified and slain. All this is true. And yet, since the day when all Judah and the inhabitants of Jerusalem did honour to Hezekiah at his death, it has been, and is, true that the great heart of humanity is generous in appreciation and honour to the name and memory of the man who has lived a noble and useful life. The scene of Thursday last at Dr. Cochrane's funeral was an object lesson on the point at issue, and an impressive revelation of the hold he had on the affectionate regards of the people of this city. Could a vision of it have been presented to him while he was yet in life, none could have had more difficulty than himself in realizing all it meant ; and I verily believe that most persons are valued and beloved far more than they themselves are accustomed to think. Yes, my friend, hearts that at times you may have thought cold, will be sore with heart-ache for you when you are gone. Perhaps you reply, " I wish we could have some of it before we are gone. I wish it were not so largely held in reserve till we have ceased to feel need of it, and till it can do us no good." Well, let the admission be frankly made, that life might be comforted and sweetened a great deal more than it is by friendly avowals of appreciation and honest praise; and yet it remains true that occasion is that which elicits manifestation of feeling.

The great majority of sensible people are reserved as to the manifestation of feeling. It may exist deep and strong where the indications are not obtruded on the attention of the person concerned ; but, occasion arising, the feeling will find vent and expression. And as our sense of the value of our mercies is keenest in the experience of their loss, so the death of a generous friend, a beloved pastor, a noble citizen, intensifies our sense of his worth ; and our feeling of loss seeks to find expression in honouring his name and memory. And our departed friend, Dr. Cochrane, was appreciated and beloved far beyond what he himself ever realized or imagined.

2. A life that closes at its greatest eminence of usefulness and active service gathers around its close the greatest halo of significance and public regard. Hezekiah ascended the throne in the full vigour of early manhood, and he reigned twenty-nine years. Hence his reign and his life terminated while his powers of mind and body were in unabated vigour, and his service to the nation was at its best. Being

in the highest degree a potent factor in the national
life, the blank made by his death was most impres-
sively felt, and the shock of it sent a thrill of sorrow
through the whole nation. So has it been in the case
of him whose eminent services and departed worth
we seek to-day to honour. The point of eminence
which Dr. Cochrane had reached was possible of
attainment only through a long series of years of
efficient and distinguished usefulness ; and at that
point of eminence it closed. A peaceful, green old age
in retirement from active labour is the dream of many.
To make provision for it they toil, and plan, and fret
themselves. In how very few cases is that dream ever
realized ! No fond dream of that nature was
cherished by your late pastor. Enthusiasm for work
was the reigning passion of his life ; rest, he could not.
In work he found his pleasure ; out of work he could
not live. Retirement from it had no attraction. Working overtime, regarded by many as a hardship, was
no hardship for him. Whence all that enthusiasm for
work ? Whence the inspiration of that busy life ?
What was the secret motive power of all that
activity ? Was it not this—that he had in him so
much of the spirit of the Master Himself, who could
say, " My meat is to do the will of him that sent me,
and to finish his work." Every hour of his day of
labour was fully filled, even to the going down of the

sun, and his day has closed with a most impressive sunset.

Ever in the public eye as a necessity of the work he was doing, and admired for the versatility that enabled him to carry on so many and diverse lines of service, the regards not merely of this city, but of all parts of the province and Dominion, have gathered around his death. His passing away at his best, in the midst of his abounding labours, has lent intensity to the shock which his death has sent abroad throughout the Church and the Dominion.

Who does not feel that such a death serves, in the plan of God, like the translation of Elijah, to intensify our sense of man's immortality? The shroud of mystery hanging over the disappointing death of Moses, the man of God, in the land of Moab, by the Jordan, becomes cleared away as we see him long centuries afterwards on the Mount of Transfiguration with Christ. The plan of God in the grand life of that great leader of Israel comes out more fully, and the fragment of it seen at Nebo is justified when discovered to have connection with this other fragment, of which a glimpse is seen on the holy mount ; as we take in the vision of the transfiguration scene, and discover that he who, debarred from Canaan, died in Moab, has now come from heaven to meet with Christ on the holy mount.

A grand and noble life, broken off at its best, presents on its earthly side an aspect of disappointing incompleteness; but this arises from our limited range of vision, and our failure to include the unseen, the invisible and eternal. When we see in the clearer light of the by-and-bye we shall feel constrained to exclaim, "He hath done all things well."

3. Such lives of good and great men in Church and state are gifts from God of unspeakable value. What is it that makes a great and noble nation? not territorial extent or vast population. China has these and is falling to pieces. Not powerful warships and iron-clads. China has these also, but she lacks men—men to man them, men inspired with love of country, men of commanding and administrative ability, men in sympathy with enlightened ideas, men worthy of national confidence. Men of noble character make the noble nation. And as God builds up and blesses the nation through good men, so does He build up and bless His Church. He sends men to arouse, inspire and lead the Church to holy effort; and a revived activity in the cause of Christ blesses those in whom the new impulse is awakened, and blesses those in whose behalf it is evoked. In a very marked degree you, as a congregation, have been blessed with such a messenger and man of God. Remember the fervour and power with which the Gospel has been

preached to you from this pulpit during the past thirty-six years. Remember the burning earnestness of appeal to heart and conscience, as he sought to arouse you to nobler service. Remember his pleadings with the unconverted. Who can estimate the impress of his life upon this city? But we must not limit our survey of his life to the city in which he lived. Canada is better, and purer, and nobler to-day because he lived in it. In a preëminent degree he led in sending Gospel ordinances into its new townships and remote settlements. With forcible eloquence he pleaded the claims of Home Missions, in Church Courts and from the pulpit, on both sides of the Atlantic, winning the admiration of those to whose liberality he made appeal, and the gratitude of those whom he helped to bless with the public means of grace. His name will long be remembered in connection with Home Missions throughout the Dominion.

To myself his death is a great personal loss. We were born the same year, I being just one month his senior. For thirty-six years past we have been most intimately associated together in the Presbytery and in general Church work. I have stood by his coffin, I have taken part in his funeral, and I am now conducting this memorial service, and yet, somehow, it all appears to me like a dream, and I cannot realize that he has gone.   But my true, my trusted and beloved friend of so many years is gone.   The blank made by his death to me, personally, may remain as it is ; but this vacant pulpit and vacant pastorate must be filled.   Pray to God to send you a man of his own choosing, a man of God, mighty in the Scriptures, a worthy successor to him to whose name and memory we this day so worthily attach the epitaph of Judah's pious reforming King : " And Hezekiah slept with his fathers, and they buried him in the chiefest of the sepulchres of the sons of David ; and all Judah and the inhabitants of Jerusalem did him honour at his death."

REMINISCENCES BY PROFESSOR BRYCE, LL.D.

My knowledge of Dr. Cochrane goes back to his coming to Brantford, in 1862, I being a native of the Brantford District.   Coming to a congregation which had been organized for some years, Rev. Wm. Cochrane, in the very vigour of his manhood, at once took a strong hold of the community, and became much sought for in the county and Presbytery to which I belonged,   My first marked recollection of him is at one of the social gatherings held in the congregation of Mt. Pleasant.   It seems to have been in the year 1869, in the year that he was preparing to visit the Old Country.   His address that evening was vigorous and impressive.   At that time I remember he asked me, a young theological student, to be *locum tenens* for him in Zion Church, during his absence; but I had previously accepted another appointment.

My connection with Mr. Cochrane was, however, very intimate after my appointment to Winnipeg in 1871.   In 1872 he became Convener of the Assembly's Home Mission Committee, and for twenty-seven years I had most intimate connection with him, having been associated with Home Missions during the whole period.   Many important problems connected with the opening up of the North-Western prairies were discussed by us in what was from first to last a very large correspondence.   He was always a prompt and satisfactory correspondent.   His methodical attention to all his work was something remarkable. I remember being in his study and his remarking to me that he could tell whether a book had been displaced during his absence, and this surprising mastery of detail he carried out in all his work.   Of course his being Convener, and responsible for the supply of funds, and hence for the cutting down of grants, and my being an agent, seeing the great wants of our West, and so largely engaged in spending the Home Mission money (I trust always judiciously), led to many a divergence of opinion and interest. Both of us, too, had, I presume, a good supply of the "*Per-fervidum ingenium scotorum*," but with it all we had no serious difficulties, and were always friendly and on the best of terms.

The proposal to change Manitoba College from Kildonan to Winnipeg, in 1873, led to Dr. Cochrane being sent up to Manitoba for the first time. That was an important event. It represented the conflict —the inevitable conflict—between the old and the new, between sentiment and reason. Dr. Black was present at the General Assembly of 1873, and the Assembly sympathized much with the old pioneer, but the brethren saw the necessity of change in the College site. Accordingly Dr. Ure, an old friend of Dr. Black, and Dr. Cochrane, representing the younger element of the Church, were appointed a commission to go to Manitoba to deal with the matter. They came, met with Presbytery, talked with the people, and saw what needed to be done. The matter was practically settled in a very out-of-the-way place, of which I have never before given an account. One of the Commissioners went to Portage la Prairie, and was returning; the other was going out. In those days it was by stage or conveyance. I accompanied one of them, and we met at a half-way inn between Winnipeg and Portage la Prairie, and there, late into the night, discussed all the facts of the case which the commissioners had gathered.

They decided, as is well known, that in the following year the College should be transferred to Winnipeg.

Dr. Cochrane was very busy in Winnipeg and elsewhere in the province preaching and obtaining information about the country. He had many friends in the new city. He performed marriages—I presume they were all legal, but our law was in a very uncertain state then. All have since been made legal at any rate.

Knox Church, Winnipeg, was just rising into note, having some fifty members, and gave then promise of the strength and zeal it has since shown. It was necessary to have a settled pastor, and it will be remembered that Dr. Cochrane was the first choice, and was actually called by the congregation. He did not see his way to come, but ever after had a strong interest in the mother church of Winnipeg. The matters, by detail, of his dealing with the Missions will be, I am sure, much more accurately given in Dr. Cochrane's diary than in any statement I could make. One other important matter however should be mentioned, that is, the establishment of Theology in Manitoba College. Manitoba College had, with the permission of the General Assembly, given instruction to students under the jurisdiction of the Presbytery of Manitoba.   It was deemed wise to have the College made a theological College.   In addition to this the collapse of the boom in Winnipeg and Manitoba lands had seriously injured the financial standing of many of the people of the city and province.   The College building, with lands and all, costing about $40,000, had lately been erected.   One subscription of $11,000 had been rendered practically valueless, and though the College was then the leading College in numbers and prestige in Manitoba, yet the financial problem was a serious one.   To meet this it was thought a prominent man from the East with strong eastern connection should be got, who would act as Principal and Professor of Theology.   Dr. Cochrane was spoken of by many, and though there was no assurance that he would accept the position, yet he was most favourably thought of.   In the end, Rev. Dr. King, of Toronto, was chosen to fill the position.

Dr. Cochrane had numerous visits to the West, and was always welcome there.   His visit to British Columbia in connection with the taking over of the churches which had formerly belonged to the Church of Scotland was one of his most important missions. I remember being in Victoria at the time that St. Andrew's Church, the chief Church of Scotland congregation, came to a decision to join the Presbyterian

Church in Canada. At that time I remember well hearing of the part Dr. Cochrane had taken in the negotiations for bringing about the happy result.

Dr. Cochrane's place will be hard to fill. He was a most valuable member of any deliberative body. He was quick, clear headed and persuasive. He had a great power of work and much facility in managing troublesome matters. Long will his well-known voice and willing help be missed at meetings of the brethren.

***

Reminiscences by Dr. McMullen.

Our friends are more to us than we realize while they are with us, and the strength of the bond binding us to them becomes discovered in the breaking. The death of Dr. Cochrane has made a great blank in my life. The threads forming the bond of friendship between us were numerous. Born in the same year, and only a month apart, we commenced the race of life together; and from the time of his settlement in Brantford in 1862, for thirty-six years we ran the race together. Our views were in general accord upon almost all subjects. We were often together on committee work of Presbytery, Synod and General Assembly. When deputations had to be sent to settle Church troubles that had broken out within the

"VANDUARA."

(Dr. Cochrane's Residence in Brantford.)

bounds of Presbytery or Synod, we generally were on such deputations.   I had thus most ample opportunity of seeing Dr. Cochrane's real character, gifts and ability tested and exemplified.   He possessed most admirable gifts for harmonizing differences, and bringing alienated parties to agreement.   He took a broad, generous view of a case, and courageously asserted and stood by the just and the right.   The influence of personal friendship never warped his judgment, or abated his emphasis in asserting and insisting on what was dutiful and proper between contending parties.   He was manly and fearless in speaking out what he believed to be right.   Nor was he hasty in arriving at conclusions or forming a judgment.   But my recollections of Dr. Cochrane, gathered from private intercourse throughout thirty-six years, are much more pleasant and sacred than any I have referred to for the purpose of illustrating how his strength of character and sterling worth impressed me and commanded ever-increasing confidence.   I was a constant guest at his house when the Presbytery met in Brantford, as he was at mine when we met in Woodstock.   I knew him as thoroughly as any brother minister could—in conversation at the family table, in devotion at the family altar, and in the privacy of his study—and every recollection of him I possess is pleasant and happy, and befitting his

17

character as a devout man of God. He was of vastly higher type, spiritually, than slight acquaintance with him might suggest. Being an efficient leader among men wherever he appeared, his ready manner and other characteristics might suggest to the eye of a stranger that he was self-assertive and ambitious. But what does such admission amount to but this: that he did not wholly escape the risk to which every one who leads is exposed. Those who knew him best held him in highest appreciation, and in this is furnished the most conclusive testimony to the genuine worth and devout character of the man. His memory is an inspiration to myself. He being dead yet speaketh. I seem at times to hear his familiar voice, and to see his familiar face and form. So real and so near does he seem to be that imagination beguiles fact, and fact seems but imagination. Yet he is gone, and the shock of his sudden death gives emphasis to the duty of showing to our friends in every suitable way, while they are yet with us, the tender regard in which we hold them. There is in this world a vast amount of genuine unrevealed appreciation and affection that, just as well as not, might brighten and bless human life, did those who treasure it only imitate the example of the woman who, instead of reserving the box of precious ointment for the Saviour's burial, anointed Him with it as He sat at meat.

It falls to the lot of comparatively few persons to receive from their friends and associates so many and varied marks and expressions of appreciation and regard as Dr. Cochrane was favoured with ; and yet who that knows the work and the worth of the man so suddenly called away can suppress the wish that the wide-spread affection and honour in which he was held, as evinced at his death, could have been more fully understood and realized by him when the consciousness of it would have cheered and gladdened him unspeakably amid the arduous difficulties of his noble and trying labours. Long will his name and memory be held in honour and affection among his brethren.

CHAPTER X.

SERMONS.

A S already stated, this sermon was prepared by
Dr. Cochrane the week before his death :

The Pilgrims Song.

Brantford Octr 16th 1898   Psalm 119. V 54.

*" Thy statutes have been my songs in the house of
my pilgrimage."*

Singing is the worship of angels. At the creation
the morning stars sang together, and all the sons of
God shouted for joy. They announced the advent, a
multitude of the heavenly host praising God ; and
they celebrate the finished work of redemption in
heaven, the voice of many angels saying : "Worthy
is the Lamb that was slain to receive power and
riches and wisdom and strength, and honour and
glory and blessing." Joy, rejoice, sing, praise, exult
and exalt His name, are frequent expressions found
in Old Testament Scriptures.

The Jewish people were full of song. Many of
their songs were of a warlike character, intended for

the battlefield, or after the achievement of victories, such as the passage of the Red Sea (Exodus xv.) and Deborah's song (Judges v.). The march to Canaan furnished them with abundant themes for song, and after their settlement in the land praise and song were assiduously cultivated. The service of song in the temple was a prominent part in their worship, while "Songs of Degrees," "Songs in the Night," and "Songs of Deliverance" marked important events in the experience of the individual and the nation. Such was often the custom of the Apostolic Church (Acts ii. 46, 47). Exhortations to song abound in the epistles (Ephesians v. 19 ; Colossians iii. 16). This is also the work of the redeemed in glory; the new song, the song of the redeemed, and the song of Moses and the Lamb, make heaven's arches ring with continuous praise. David, the sweet singer of Israel by preëminence, has furnished the Church of God with a storehouse of song adapted to every emergency of life. He frequently compares himself to a pilgrim. His psalms give us the secret of his cheerful state of mind. "Thy statutes have been my songs in the house of my pilgrimage." It was the custom in the East for the traveller, when he halted for the night in some inn, which was for the time being the house of his pilgrimage, to take up the lyre, or some instrument of music, and soothe himself with a song of love, or war, or romance. Stroll-ing bands of minstrels in Switzerland often enliven the night and cheer the stranger by their national melodies. In olden times it was the custom to versify the laws, that the people might learn them by heart and sing them. This idea seems implied in the lan-guage of the text. God's testimonies had been so familiar to him, and so much beloved, that he sang them ; they were the joy and rejoicing of his heart.

The theme of David's song was the statutes or law of God. It is spoken of in the most exalted terms in Scripture, notably in Psalm xix. 7-10. Its purity, permanence and perfection are repeatedly referred to in Psalm cxix. This law was his boast, his medi-tation, his delight. It cheered him in solitude, sup-ported him in trial, and directed him in perplexity.

The phrase, " house of my pilgrimage " includes two thoughts :

(*a*) The body he inhabited was only temporary. It is spoken of in Scripture (2 Cor. v. 1). Like the tabernacle on the march, it was fitted for its present purpose, but would give place to a more permanent fabric.

(*b*) His life on earth was but a pilgrimage. Shorter or longer, this was not his rest. He was simply on his way home, where were his Saviour, his friends, and his imperishable possessions.

The Christian, above all men, should possess this happy frame of mind. Religion ought not to be gloomy. The book of Psalms alone, not to speak of other portions of God's Word, has been a wonderful source of strength to believers in all ages. What has been said of the hundredth Psalm, "the grand old Puritan anthem, full of the breath of the Lord, consoling and comforting many," may be said of all. Their music is adapted to every voice. Singing songs on life's rough road is a blessed employment and a hopeful sign. It makes the road seem shorter, relieves the tediousness of the way. Going up to Jerusalem, the tribes cheered themselves by song. It shows that the journey is coming to an end, and the traveller anticipating the home greetings that await him. The Christian's song is pitched on a higher key than David's, to whom the incarnated love of God was a thing of faith. He can sing of redeeming love in nobler strains.

> " I will sing for Jesus,
>   With His blood He bought me,
> And all along my pilgrim way
>   His loving hand has brought me.
>
> " I will sing for Jesus,
>   His name alone prevailing,
> Shall be my sweetest music
>   When heart and pulse are failing."

The sweetest song that the great composer Mozart ever sang was his last—"The Requiem." He had been employed in this exquisite piece for several weeks, his soul filled with inspiration of the richest melody, and already claiming kindred with immortality. After giving it its last touch, and breathing into it that undying spirit of song which was to consecrate it through all times as the " Circean strain," he fell into a gentle and quiet slumber. At length the light footsteps of his daughter awoke him. "Come hither," said he, "my Emilie; my task is done ; my requiem is finished." " Say not so, dear father," said the gentle girl, interrupting him with tears in her eyes. "You must be better ; you look better, for even now your cheek has a glow on it. I am sure we shall nurse you well again. Let me bring you something refreshing." " Do not deceive yourself, my love," said the dying father; "this wasted form can never be restored by human aid. From heaven's mercy alone do I look for help in this my dying hour. You spoke of refreshment, my little Emilie. Take these my last notes ; sit down by my piano here ; sing with them the hymn of your sainted mother ; let me once more hear those tones which have been so long my solace and delight." Emilie obeyed, and with a voice enriched with the tenderest emotion, sang the following stanzas :

" Spirit, thy labour is o'er,
Thy term of probation is run,
Thy steps are now bound for the untrodden shore,
And the race of immortals begun.

" Spirit, look not on the strife,
Or the pleasures of life with regret—
Pause not at the threshold of limitless life
To mourn for the day that is set.

" Spirit, no fetters can bind,
No wicked have powers to molest ;
There the weary, like thee—the wretched shall find
A heaven, a mansion of rest.

" Spirit, how bright is the road,
For which thou art now on the wing,
Thy home it will be, with thy Saviour and God,
Their loud hallelujah to sing."

As she concluded, she dwelt for a moment on the low, melancholy notes of the piece, and then, turning from the instrument, looked in silence for the approving smile of her father. It was the still and passionless smile which the rapt and joyous spirit left, with the seal of death, upon those features. How sweet to pass away on the wings of sacred joy, to take our place in the celestial choir who praise day and night !

The following sermon was prepared by Dr. Cochrane on the Saturday before his death, and was intended for the Sabbath evening service :

If need be.

Brantford Octr. 16. 1898.   1st Peter 1st V6.

" Wherein ye greatly rejoice, though now for a season, if need be, ye are in heaviness through manifold temptations."

Although it may not be the prominent thought in the mind of the Apostle when he wrote these words, it is a truth taught us in God's Word, that there is a "need be," in all our trials and afflictions. Nothing happens fortuitously, accidentally, or unforeseen by our Heavenly Father. Every providential event is absolutely necessary for our progress and sanctification. We may not often believe this—often it is hard to think so ; but the fact remains, independent of the measure of faith we give it. When visiting homes of sickness and bereavement, we endeavour to soothe the broken-hearted and bereaved by saying that everything is well and wisely ordered. But when it falls to our own lot to bear similar chastisement, we do not accept the comfort we have offered others in the same circumstances. If we do not say in so many words that we have been hardly dealt with above others, we feel it ; if we do not call in question the justice of God's dealings, we think that compared with others, who seem exempted from such heavy chastisements and sorrows, we have good cause to murmur. Like Jonah, when the gourd withered, we say : " It is better for us to die than to live." Because our poor reason cannot comprehend the why and wherefore of our allotments, we become restive and querulous, when God's dealings with us are the very best adapted to our spiritual wants.

The "need be" for chastisement is, in many cases, obvious. To increase our longings after heaven, to lessen our devotion to the world, to qualify us for the fellowship of the pure and their exalted employments, to test our faith and strengthen our trust and confidence in God—these and such like are the gracious ends God has in view in earthly afflictions. The "need be " often extends over a large portion of our existence, for we do not always recognize God's hand in our chastisements.

Secondary causes are frequently laid hold of to account for untoward events. We lament the absence of this precaution, or the neglect of this duty, and endeavour in every possible way to account for our evil fortune, independent of that God without whose knowedge not even a sparrow falls to the ground. Thus we try hard " to push God out of our concerns," as if our happiness, our health, and our worldly prosperity were matters entirely under our own control. Now, while such a state of mind continues, there is a " need be " that the chastisement should be continued and increased in severity. We must be brought to feel that in no case does affliction spring from the ground, that it is the Lord who takes away as well as gives. Not until this feeling is developed do we profit by affliction.

Nay, we ought, if possible, to understand why the particular calamity has been sent upon us. Much has been gained when we honestly recognize our Heavenly Father's hand in all our earthly ills and evils, but much more would be gained if we could put our finger upon the special sin which He intends to correct and remove, for God's infinite wisdom is never more clearly seen than in adapting His dealings to our necessities. It is not enough for us to say, " I was dumb, I opened not my mouth because Thou didst it." " It is the Lord, let Him do what seemeth Him good."

We should find out the special lesson He intends us to learn. The physician endeavours to make his treatment bear directly upon that part of the body which is diseased. He probes the wound and applies remedies or performs certain surgical operations that have a direct bearing upon the malady. And so does the Almighty, when He would destroy some secret sin or punish some flagrant act of backsliding which endangers our whole spiritual nature. Unless, therefore, we are driven by His dealing with us to examine our feelings and purposes and the entire tenor of our life, we fail to receive the profit intended. Time, I grant you, is required before the child of God can understand or acquiesce in all the "need be's" that mark his brief existence upon earth. The ways of the Almighty are at all times past finding out exhaustively, and can never be traced by mortals hastily. But in looking back at the past, with all its severe and successive ills, do we not all feel that every separate act of discipline was imperatively demanded for the welfare of our souls? When that beloved child was taken, the pride of the household, and the idol of your affection, you saw nothing in the bereavement but an act of God's sovereignty, most arbitrary and uncalled for. It was a long time before you could bow to the dispensation or believe that there was a wise necessity for such a bitter grief. When by industry and diligence you had gained a competency in life, and looked forward to the time when you could rest from the toils and struggles of business, you saw your goods and possessions swept away in a moment and fall into the hands of dishonourable rivals. You were almost driven to despair, and felt as if justice and judgment were no longer the habitation of God's throne. And yet there was a " need be " for this sad and sudden reverse of fortune. You did not see it then, for at best our spiritual discernment is weak ; but in the light of revolving years, and with an enlarged and correct comprehension of dangers that then surrounded you, you are now convinced that but for such a visitation your state would have been awful as regards eternity.

> " Days of fever and of fretting,
>   Hours of kind and blessed calm,
>   Moods of sinking, when the spirit,
>   Overstrained, is downward borne ;
>   Moods of soaring, when our being
>   Springs elastic to the morn ;
>   With these is life begun and closed ;
>   Of these its strange mosaic composed."

Now, the text is designed for those who have such seasons of heaviness. They are part of the programme of life. They form an important element of spiritual discipline. It is not intended that God's people should always be jubilant and joyous. There must be periods when they are forced to weep bitter tears, and almost sink under the heavy burdens, when they bend like the willows under the stormy blast.

Many regard this heaviness of spirit as a blemish, as entirely out of place in a believer, especially one who has made attainments in the divine life. They imagine that faith should overcome all despondency, and question the reality of the spiritual life in those who are frequently cast down. But is such a conclusion warranted? Have not the best of saints occasions when they are low-spirited and cheerless and sad, and when they cannot enjoy with keen relish the ordinances of religion? It would be indeed very wonderful if they did. Possibly they have just recovered from a severe and prolonged sickness, which has left its effects on both mind and body; or they have been called to part with their nearest and dearest friend on earth, or have been bereaved of children, or have just passed through a long series of crushing disappointments, almost sufficient to overturn the reason and induce despair. For what purpose, let me ask, have such afflictions been sent? Not simply that the sufferers should see the rod, but feel it; not simply that they should drink the cup of gall, but taste its bitterness; not simply to die to sin, but to realize all the pangs of crucifixion. Chastisement does not serve its end unless it leaves an impression upon the character. The chastisements sent were just what your condition demanded, and, guided by a loving hand, they produced the desired end, while grace sustained you under the shock. In view, then, of your past experience, are you not willing to leave the disposal of all your affairs for the future in the hand of God?   If so much mercy and wisdom have mingled with all your past afflictions, are you not prepared to place yourself unreservedly under his control? Whether your days on earth be brief or prolonged, depend upon it there will be many "need be's" demanding all the patient submission of which your nature is capable. Nay, it may be, requiring a stronger faith in the justice and goodness of God than you have yet been called upon to exercise. In prospect of such unforeseen trials, cherish a firm and abiding belief in the unerring ordinations of heaven, saying :

> " Not to my wish, but to my want,
>   Do Thou Thy gifts supply ;
> Unasked, what good thou knowest, grant ;
>   What ill, though asked, deny."

But there is another thought contained in the text. Not only is there a "need be" for our manifold temptations and trials, but there is a "need be" for our heaviness under temptations and trials. The early Christians, to whom the Apostle wrote, were heroic, courageous to the last degree. They took joyfully the spoiling of their goods. They did not murmur because of persecution and reproach. But, while the general current of their lives was happy, there were, doubtless, times when they experienced gloom and melancholy. It was not always sunshine. There were dark days in their history, when faith held the promises by a weaker grasp. It was so even with the Apostle Paul, in spite of his buoyancy and unquenchable ardour. He describes his life as one of alternate sadness and gladness. "As unknown, yet well known; as dying, yet alive; as chastened, but not killed; as sorrowful, yet always rejoicing; as poor, yet making many rich; as having nothing, yet possessing all things?" And is this not the experience of most Christians? forcing us, perhaps, to cry like Job, "The arrows of the Almighty are within me, the poison thereof drinketh up my spirit, the terrors of God do set themselves in array against me. Have pity upon me, O ye my friends, for the hand of God hath touched me." This erroneous idea, that heaviness of spirit is sinful, is strengthened by the unwise counsel of friends. They teach that just as soon as possible we are to forget our losses and get away from the presence of those things that call up the memory of bereavements. Going out into society and engaging in employments of an exciting nature are often recommended to beat out the remembrance of bitter griefs. "Make an effort," says some strong-minded one, who has never passed through the furnace. "Don't yield to melancholy; rouse yourself from this dormancy of feeling and action ; do not sit and mourn as if no others in the world had shared such misery." How foolish is such language addressed to the broken and bleeding heart? Pass on your way, ye strong-hearted ones, whose souls have never been lacerated. You cannot sympathize with the sufferer's groans ; your presence but exasperates and increases the mental torture. "The Christian who knows the agony of conflict, who has felt storms unloosed in his own heart, whom doubt has scorched and remorse has gnawed, let such an one draw near. He is one of my fellows. Where I fall he has faltered. The hand that reaches out to me trembles still. His weakness gives me strength. Stooping in the dust beside me, he lifts me in lifting himself." But it may be asked, Why is there a "need be" for this heaviness? If we had no answer, it is sufficient to say that God, in His infinite wisdom, has so willed it. He who formed the human soul, and knows the peculiar sensibility and delicacy of its emotions, has made grief and tears an outlet against despair. But, further, were there no such periods in our history, some of the most delightful experiences of the sanctified soul would be altogether unknown. The glory and excellence of the Divine Being are not always nor only seen from mountain tops like Pisgah, or Tabor, or Hermon.

Other manifestations equally valuable are to be witnessed in Gethsemane around the Cross. In solitude and gloom the promises acquire new meaning, and the soul is brought into a nearness of contact with the Divine Being not possible in times of gladness. And need I remind the stricken mourner that the Lord Jesus Christ, during His earthly sojourn, was preëminently a man of sorrows and acquainted with grief? The heaviness of His heart was for the most part suppressed and hidden from common observation, so that in the bitterest moments of His history the calm current of his life seemed undisturbed. But there were occasions when it was otherwise. Hear Him amid the gloom and terrors of Gethsemane : " My soul is exceeding sorrowful, even unto death; tarry ye here and watch with me." And, again, a little afterwards, as He falls on His face praying, " O my Father, if it be possible, let this cup pass from me ; nevertheless not as I will, but as thou wilt." And still a second time, when the billows of the Divine wrath rolled over Him : " O, my Father, if this cup may not pass from me, except I drink it, thy will be done."

In the words of the prophet Jeremiah, personifying the calamities that were soon to fall upon Jerusalem, we seem to hear the Saviour exclaim : " Is it nothing to you, all ye that pass by?   Behold, and see if there be any sorrow like unto my sorrow which is done unto me, wherewith the Lord hath afflicted me in the day of his fierce anger."   Surely, then, it is not strange that believers should be subject to depression and melancholy.   They must be like the Master in His hours of humiliation as well as exaltation.   They must walk through Gethsemanes of darkness and horror ere they enter the rapturous delights of heaven.

But this heaviness is only for a season. " Weeping may endure for a night, but joy cometh in the morning."   " The ransomed of the Lord shall return and come to Zion with songs and everlasting joy upon their heads ; they shall obtain joy and gladness, and sorrow and sighing shall flee away."   The disciples were in great sadness when Jesus was about to leave them, but He gave them the promise that the abiding presence of the Holy Spirit would chase away their gloom and produce a joy before unknown. " Verily, verily, I say unto you, that ye shall weep and lament, and ye shall be sorrowful, and your sorrow shall be turned into joy.   Ye now, therefore, have sorrow, but I will see you again, and your heart shall rejoice, and your joy no man taketh from you."   And so shall it be with suffering saints when Jesus comes again.

" No more heart pangs of sadness,
When Jesus comes ;
All peace, and joy, and gladness,
When Jesus comes ;
All doubts and fears will vanish,
When Jesus comes ;
All gloom His face will banish,
When Jesus comes."

Life at the longest is but brief, and our sorrow
cannot survive it. In that bright world whither we
are hasting, all cause for melancholy is removed.
There are no tears to dim the vision of the redeemed.
The last sigh, the last pang, the last regret, ends with
expiring nature.

" High in yonder realms of light
Dwell the raptured saints above ;
Pilgrims in this vale of tears,
Once they knew, like us below,
Gloomy doubts, distressing fears,
Torturing pain, and heavy woe.

But these days of weeping o'er,
Past this scene of toil and pain,
They shall feel distress no more,
Never, never weep again."

Nor is it to be forgotten that these periods of
heaviness often precede the sunshine and the joy. It
was when the Saviour was on the eve of victory that

His soul was shrouded in darkness. It was when nearing His conquest over Satan and the powers of darkness, that He cried out, " Eloi, Eloi, lama sabacthani." " My God, my God, why hast thou forsaken me?" Just before the Christian, as described in the Pilgrim's Progress, put off his mortal garments and entered the Celestial City, a great darkness and horror fell upon him, so that he could not see before him. The sorrows of death compassed him ; he was possessed with most distressing fear that he would never obtain entrance at the gate. It was all that Hopeful could do to cheer his sinking soul, by telling him that his troubles and distresses were no sign that God had forsaken him, but rather sent to try his faith and see whether in these moments of danger he would call to mind God's former goodness.

It was even so, as Hopeful said, for in a little while Christian's heaviness gave place to courageous joy, and they entered the city in raiment that shone like gold, with crowns of honour upon their heads, and palms of victory and harps of praise within their hands. It is so still in the experience of many of God's saints. Satan puts forth his last effort to disturb their peace and cloud their vision, and to some extent succeeds. The closing eyes seem destitute of that supernatural brilliancy which in other cases illumines the dying chamber. But what of it. The darkest hour precedes the dawn. The storm reaches its greatest height before the calm. "Our light affliction, which is but for a moment, worketh for us a far more exceeding and eternal weight of glory." If then we are the children of God, we must have seasons of heaviness. They belong to the Christian life. They are necessary to our growth in piety, and are preliminary to our entering upon the permanent peace and undisturbed calm of heaven. Further, these seasons of heaviness, as they often precede, so just as frequently they follow, periods of unusual joy. These early Christians, of whom the apostles wrote, rejoiced in the prospect of an inheritance incorruptible, and undefiled, and that fadeth not away, and in the knowledge that they were kept by God through faith unto salvation ; but their rejoicing was followed by heaviness by reason of manifold temptations. It is so still in Christian experience. He who is one moment on the crest of the billow is the next moment in the trough of the sea, at the mercy of the angry elements. The intervals between the highest happiness and the most excessive griefs are brief, like to the swift translation of the soul from the weariness of time to the effulgent splendours of eternity. Blessed are they who mourn, for they shall be comforted ; who are broken in spirit, for they shall exult and sing. It is thus that they obtain permanent victory over the ills of life, and are enabled to meet death without dismay as the messenger of love.

THE LATE MRS. WATT.

That there is "a need be," in the removal from this Church—from her home and many sorrowing friends—of Mrs. William Watt, jr., who, a month ago to-day, sat with us, a silent but interested and humble disciple at the table of her Lord, we cannot doubt. We dare not call in question the wisdom of a loving Father, who, having purified her in the fiery furnace, until the image was perfect, took her home to rest and rejoice with the redeemed.   Not to exalt unduly her many virtues and graces, but to magnify the grace of God that made her what she was, and incite others to live so that they may die her death, prompts us to a simple record of her life and sufferings.

Mrs. Watt was born in a religious home, and surrounded from infancy with all those elements that contribute to the formation of a strong, attractive and gracious character.   She gave herself early to the Lord, and that her profession was genuine her entire life afterwards proved.   Like many others—and these are, as a rule, the best members in our churches—her conversion was not due to some special agency, but the necessary result of inborn piety.   Children accustomed to devotional habits, the reading of the Bible at the family altar, and catechetical instruction in their homes, seldom wander in forbidden paths. And, therefore, what she was as a girl she followed out in her own home as a mother. Her conduct was ever such as became a sincere Christian. She was naturally cheerful and of a sunny temperament, yet serious and sober-minded as occasion demanded. It was never difficult for any one to conclude whether the gay and giddy world and its pleasures, or the society of the godly, was her preference. She loved to associate with those that feared God and thought upon His name, and her happiest moments were those when, directly or indirectly, she was serving the Master whom she loved.

In the missionary schemes of the Church, and those departments that naturally fall to Christian women, she took an active part, until, in the providence of God, she was laid aside from work that she greatly enjoyed. How great the disappointment, and how sad she must have felt, when she could do little more than look on, and listen to others, we cannot imagine. Milton, when stricken with blindness, expresses the feelings of many of God's saints, when they are laid aside in the midtime of their days by diseases that baffle the skill of physicians and the assiduous atten-tion of unselfish affection :

" When I consider how my life is spent
    Ere half my days in this dark world and wide,
    And that one talent, which is death to hide,
    Lodged with me useless, though my soul more bent
    To serve therewith my Master—
    I fondly ask :
    Doth God exact day labour, light denied ?

    But patience, to prevent
    That murmur, soon replies : " God doth not need
    Either man's work, or his own gifts ; who best
    Bear his mild yoke, they serve him best ; his state
    Is kingly ; thousands at his bidding speed
    And post o'er land and ocean without rest ;
    They also serve, who only stand and wait."

God took from our beloved sister, not the organ of
sight, but that of speech, accompanied by physical
pain and weakness which, to anyone but such as she
was, must have been hard to bear.   While we cannot
fully interpret her feelings through those nine long
years of silence, this much we are warranted in saying,
that she never rebelled nor felt but there was some
good end in her being singled out to bear such a
heavy burden, and spend so many dark and weary
days and nights, ere she entered the valley that led to
the rest of the Celestial City, and was enrolled with
the saints who shout and sing.   She is not the only
one in this congregation laid aside for years, and it
may be the portion of others who shall by patient

waiting, more than active service, gain the crown. This is the noblest grace. It is easier to work than wait. The host of Israel found it far harder to walk round Jericho seven days, than to fight, and yet this seemingly singular march carried out God's designs better than by fighting, for, as the Apostle says, in the contest such trials of faith " are much more precious than of gold that perisheth, though it be tried with fire." As the angels stand and wait, so, in long seasons of bodily suffering, " when usefulness is forbidden by the jarred and thrilling nerves," we learn that our Elder Brother is with us, and never wearies of our incapacity and inability to serve him. Patience and meek submission to God's will, however mysterious it may be, and evident, though speechless, desire for the glory of God, are of mighty value in this age of eagerness and excitement. As the poet says :

> " Count each affliction, whether light or grave,
> God's messenger sent down to thee.
> Do thou with courtesy receive him."

And thus the helpless, incurable invalid, the dumb or paralyzed sister or brother, may in their solitude be doing more for the Master than the busy toiler or the eloquent preacher.

> " No act falls fruitless ; none can tell
> How vast its power may be,
> Nor what results unfolded dwell
> Within it silently."

And yet to poor, short-sighted mortals such as we are, the prolonged silence and helplessness of one who was so useful, and who gave promise of still greater things, seems strange. Although she did not aspire to leadership, nor seek to command, she was possessed of such gentleness and winsomeness of manner, that, in spite of her dislike of prominence, she would have eventually attained a place second to none among her co-workers. She was wise in counsel, and her well-balanced judgment kept her from extremes in speech or action. This church, every church, wants more like her, who, while minimizing their influence and ability, prove themselves capable of the best efforts. Women who cheerfully devote their leisure hours from household duties to Church work, and who, without any pretensions to piety above their sisters, show by their regular attendance in the house of God how greatly they value the fellowship of the saints. Very seldom during these nine long years did Mrs. Watt miss a sacramental season ; and on other occasions, when strength permitted her to be taken to the house of God, she was present. At the annual Thanksgiving meetings of the missionary societies she was a silent but interested worshipper, or, if unable to attend, her offering was always sent. Voiceless she might be in the praise of the sanctuary, but she was glad when they said unto her, " Let us go into the house of the Lord."   A day in God's courts was better to her than a thousand elsewhere.

But if the loss to us as a church is great, what must it be to those who in the now desolate home— husband and children, parents, sisters and friends— who, all the more because of her long affliction, loved her with an indescribable affection?   " Our sighs were numerous, and profuse our tears, for she we lost was lovely, and we loved her much."   We may not invade the inner shrine of the death chamber, where, surrounded by loved ones, she valiantly struggled until at last " fond nature ceased its strife and let her languish into life."

The mute lips that often in the last hours gave forth weird and plaintive notes of song, meaningless to our poor comprehension, seemed in more restful moments to speak the gratitude of her heart for kindness shown, and to anticipate the last ministra- tions of loved ones, who would fain have had her stay a little longer on the earth, " a spirit ripe for heaven," as if saying :

> " Fold the hands lightly,
> Lay the head low ;
> Smooth the hair softly
> Back from the brow,
> Dear, loving ones.

> " If the lips' crimson
>   Fadeth away ;
> If the old smile hath
>   Forgotten its play
> On the cold cheek,

> " Gather yet closer,
>   With loving caress,
> So shall there linger
>   The life-warmth to bless
> Till—the good-bye.

> " Do not be mournful,
>   Do not regret,
> I'll be the first 'o'er the river,'
>   But shall not forget,
> Mine on the shore."

At last—

> " The Angel of the Covenant
> Came, and faithful to his promise stood,
> Prepared to walk with her through death's dark vale.
> And now her eyes grew bright, and brighter still,
> Too bright for us to look upon, suffused
> With many tears and closed without a cloud.
> They set, as sets the morning star, which goes
> Not down behind the darkened west, nor hides
> Obscured among the tempests of the sky,
> But melts away into the light of heaven."

What is the lesson taught us by this life and death ? That the working day may precede by many years the grave, and the evening of active life come long before the normal setting of the sun. Sudden loss of speech and physical paralysis often surprise the strong and healthy. A little clot may in a moment plug one of the blood-vessels of the brain that supply what is called the speech centre, and then there is silence. How complex is the process, and how delicately constructed are the organs by which we convey our thoughts to others! " Fearfully and wondrously made, curiously wrought," says the Psalmist, in speaking of the human frame. The orator that has entranced thousands by his burning eloquence; the songstress that has carried spellbound delighted audiences; the strong frame that has never known fatigue, may each and all in a moment, by some mysterious cause, become like the stranded wreck that is washed over by the ebb and flow of the recurring tide. "What thy hand findeth to do, do it with thy might." If we have spent our energies in God's service, and are prematurely laid aside, let us be resigned, but if we have never attempted anything for the Master, but wasted life in self-indulgence, how terrible the recollection, and how stinging the re- morse ! It is grand to continue in work until nature wears out at three-score years and ten, or four-score years, just as the leaves fall in their appointed season,

but let the day of toil end when it may, there is immortal vigour beyond. " They say," said Dr. Guthrie,
when nearing the end, " that I am growing old, because my hair is silvered and there are crow's feet on
my forehead, and my step is not so firm and elastic
as before, but they are mistaken. That is not me.
The knees are weak, but the knees are not me. The
brow is wrinkled, but the brow is not me. This is
the house I live in. But I am young, younger than I
ever was before."